Millie Mayfield

Progression

Or, The South Defended

Millie Mayfield

Progression
Or, The South Defended

ISBN/EAN: 9783337000868

Printed in Europe, USA, Canada, Australia, Japan

Cover: Foto ©Andreas Hilbeck / pixelio.de

More available books at **www.hansebooks.com**

PROGRESSION;

OR,

THE SOUTH DEFENDED.

BY

MILLIE MAYFIELD,

OF NEW ORLEANS.

———— ◆ ————

APPLEGATE & CO., PUBLISHERS,
43 MAIN STREET, CINCINNATI, O.
1860.

Dedication.

——◦o⟡o◦——

To the intelligent, reasoning, and generous thinkers among my countrymen and countrywomen—those who are willing, with unjaundiced eyes and unprejudiced opinions, to weigh the South and her Institutions in the balance of Justice, against fanaticism and error—this volume is sincerely dedicated; while it is respectfully submitted to the consideration of all believers and admirers of the monstrosities set forth in "Uncle Tom's Cabin," *et hæc omnia genera*, for the purpose of deceiving and misleading the masses.

THE AUTHOR.

(iii)

Contents.

——◦◦⦂◦⦂◦◦——

	PAGE
INTRODUCTORY	7
CREATION	16
THE EARTH	35
MAN	66
SLAVERY	103
THE SOUTH	149
VALEDICTORY	194
NOTES	211

(v)

PROGRESSION;

OR,

THE SOUTH DEFENDED.

Introductory.

YE lords of creation, bear with me, I pray,
While I point to the object that guideth my lay;
And ye, my fair sisters, my visit excuse:
Unushered I call, but ye will not refuse
To receive me with favor, when once I explain
The laudable motives that prompted my strain.
Would my pen were inspired with the pictures it
    paints,
While I bring to your notice some sinners turned
    saints !
But my goose-quill can give but the d—l his due,
And enough it will be, for the tale is " ower true."

(7)

In this age of great wonders, of "rights,"
    "ists," and " isms,"
Of social o'erturns, and political schisms;
Of miracles working right under our noses,
That shake to the center the good laws of Moses;
Of wordy tornadoes, and shrieking anathema
Pitched into our teeth and our faces, ex-cathedra,
By raving reformers, a dictating brood,
Who the laws of creation would change, if they
    could;
When the B—rs, and P—rs, and S—ds, & Co.,
With their petticoat leader, the sleek Mistress S—e!
Have emptied their vials of rancor and spleen
O'er the line, marked by Mason and Dixon, between
The South, sunny land—and " free soil!" where
    jingles
The pewter that forms their religion, which mingles
With all their vile stuff, from rank hate to alloy,
Which freely they scatter our peace to destroy,
And under the cloak of religion, sow seeds
Of discord, fast ripening to enmity's deeds,
Between the two races—whom but to befriend,
Is their motive for meddling, they vainly pretend;
Then gloat o'er the warfare their daring calls forth,

And from the cold lips of the "Rights"-ridden
    North
Boldly challenge the South to a contest of strength
In a match with opponents, whose laws have a
    length
And a breadth of their own, paramount to the
    laws
Of their country!—Then say, has any one cause
To wonder a daughter of that sunny land,
Most basely defamed by a bigoted band,
Should take up the gauntlet, defiantly hurled,
Tho' all bearded creation contemptuously curled
Their indignant mustaches, at womanly knight,
Who the seven-headed beast would thus valiantly
    fight?
Yes, land of my sires, of my home and my love!
Be mine the blest portion thy honor to prove,
Be mine the dear task to wipe off from thy brow
That plague-spot, rogues planted, which grows on
    it now,
Or their fingers of falsehood so foully have traced
Vile calumnies, ne'er to be wholly erased
Till the sense of mankind shall awake to those laws
Which govern creation.

With reverence I pause,
And a blessing I ask from the great Source of
    Light,
To hallow each axiom my heart would indite;
That truth from my pen so prophetic may roll,
As shall carry conviction to every great soul;
Conviction that God's laws, unchanging and just,
Shall abide, when weak man has resolved his to
    dust!
    And those laws. Will the P—rs, and B—rs,
        and S—es,
Who, on ill-gotten laurels so proudly repose,
Asserting, "All men are born equal!" but will
    they
Point the law in creation which proves it? or say
(Taking Scripture to back me), what meaneth the
    story,
That one star from another shall differ in glory?
Why not have them *equal*, with splendor supernal,
To shine thro' all ages, undimmed and eternal?
For one is a star, just as much as the other—
Pray, why should the one, then, outrival his
    brother?
    And again (from the Bible I freely must quote,

For pailsful of Scripture Mistress S—e sets afloat)
We are told, in that heaven are seraphs who see
The face of their Maker continually.
But it sayeth not *all* have that privilege blest,
Of the angelic dwellers of that land of rest!
Then why should that God, who made heaven and
    earth ;
From whom suns and stars claim their glorious
    birth;
Who fashioned the angels and cherubim fair,
But made them not *equal*—pause, skeptic, just
    there—
Say, why should he make an exception in man,
Or alter in him, the original plan?

   Ascending, by steps, from the lower types,
    brutes
Are marked in each species with distinct attri-
    butes
To man, walking upright, a creature, they say,
Just less than the angels—this none will gainsay,
Still, the different species of men on the earth
Must claim the prerogatives stamped them at birth;
And who will deny that to each has been given
A different glory, like stars in yon heaven?

The great laws of God show distinctions.   Each
    star,
That, with scintillant splendor, shines out from
    afar,
Was in its beginning an atom in space,
Which, step by step, circled in ne'er-ending race,
Till it shone out full-orbed, as a glorious sun,
With its satellite planets, contented, each one,
As planets to be, which with borrowed light shine,
Nor think themselves *suns* from the ray, half di-
    vine,
That lights their dark faces when touched by the
    beam
Which flows from their primary in a full stream,
But, without which, the darkness of ne'er-ending
    night,
Its somber wings folding, existence would blight.
'Tis thus in the vast book of nature we read
Great truths, far above each sectarian creed.
On its gold-illumed pages unerring we trace,
The dependence of some of the bodies of space
Upon other orbs, still ranging higher and higher,
On the grand chords harmonious of heaven's bright
    lyre ;

Then, down to the earth, where the baser strings
    grate,
No exceptions we find in this progressive state.
  As nearest the skies, take the genus called
    " homo "—
For earthly progression ranks him major-domo—
Thro' five distinct grades runs the species, de-
    scending
To that, which the good book will tell us lies end-
    ing
In Afric's warm regions of desert and palm,
First peopled by Noah's cursed son, yclept
    " Ham;"
Which, in savage condition, *one* degree from the
    brute
Is only removed.   (This, I know, will not suit
Your screamers for freedom, and clerical forces,
Who, astride of their huge black republican horses,
Would ride o'er the neck of the South, their great
    evil,
In the name of the Lord! Freddy D., and the
    d—l !)
Then down thro' creation we find, link by link,
The chain all unbroken. We adore, while we think

Of the wisdom which fashioned each creature pro-
    gressive,
From lowest type upward to man! Inexpressive
Are words in their meaning, to tell the whole
    story,
How, from man rising upward from glory to glory,
Are angels, and cherubs, and seraphim, singing
The praises of Him, in whom all had beginning!
    O Ariel! thy wing I would borrow from thee!
Puck, lend me thy girdle, while backward I flee
O'er the mountains of Time, rising hoary and gray,
Back, back to the moment when dawned the first
    day,
When the glimmer electric rent darkness apart,
And the first throb pulsated in Nature's great
    heart!
    When Deity spoke, and the darkness replied;
When his laws were established, so fixed to abide,
Till the circles of time are fulfilled on the dial,
And every created thing, pure from the trial
Which tested its faith in a fiery ordeal,
Has merged from nonentity into the real;
Has acted its part in the drama of life;
Has basked in its sunshine, and battled its strife;

Has seen, link by link, the chain part, that to
    earth
Binds the spirit, still looking for heavenly birth,
For that glorious celestial progression which love,
Love Divine, has marked out in the bright realms
    above ;
When casting behind it its fetters of clay,
The spirit, triumphant, soars on its bright way
To regions of light on the crystalline river
That laves the white throne of our life's glorious
    Giver !
Let me trace, step by step, those most wonderful
    laws
Which sprang into being when breathed the First
    Cause,
And which govern inanimate objects as well
As those warmed with life—tho' no man can tell
Why such and such causes produce their effects,
Yet that such the result is, there's no one objects.
Let me show that the present condition of man,
Is but the result of an organized plan,
By superior Intelligence fashioned and made,
Ere Time's corner-stone in creation was laid.

Creation.

THE sea of space was moteless. Systems,
  spheres,
In circling marches, marked no passing years
On Time's great dial—time was then unborn;
But, with the mild, balm-breathing, blue-eyed
  morn,
In the still womb of chaos unformed lay,
A fœtal mass, unconscious of to-day.
  The universe—the countless orbs that rise
In golden glory now o'er burnished skies,
Those stellar monarchs of the vast domains
Whose fields are glittering with planet trains,
And wandering comets, in eccentric lines,
Nearing the throne where glowing splendor shines,
And every world that's teeming now with light
And life, lay wrapt in embryonic night!
  Nonentity! O! say, what mortal eye
May with a backward glance thy depths descry—

What mortal pen may paint the somber pall
Which dropped its darkening shadows over all
The regions where glad life triumphant reigns
To-day? For once, encircled with thy chains,
Each mighty element that sweeps the deep
Lay hushed beneath thy touch in harmless sleep;
The germ of every living thing that springs,
On thy broad bosom folded silent wings—
And thro' the lofty aisles around, no sound
Broke on the solemn silence, deep, profound!

But now a pulse, like the first throb that tells
Of quickening life, thro' all thy fibers swells.
Whence comes the glow that lights thy ashen
    face,
O! dun-browed mother of a countless race
Of golden glories shining thro' all space?
Whence comes the thrill, coursing thy dark veins
    thro',
Whose speed electric wakes each throb anew
Ere it expires? The mighty Word which was
In the beginning—the great Primal Cause—
Is breathed, and lo! startling the silence round,
The fathomless abyss gives back the sound,
Reverberating thro' the caverns deep,

Wakening each atom from its pristine sleep
Out-speeding thought, it sweeps the broad aisles
    thro',
Where now each firmament hangs its bann'rol blue,
Where now each world rolls on its ceaseless way,
Each sun from slumber calls the drowsy day.
On, on, the mighty Word, with lightning march,
And spell Promethean, ignites the torch
Of electricity, to work the will
Of the Great Architect's supernal skill!

  O! mighty power! what sway to thee is given;
Thy chain, O Electricity! unriven,
Spans the wide earth, circles the walls of heaven!
There's not a leaf that trembles on the breeze—
There's not an eddy dimpling in the seas—
There's not a cloudlet floating o'er yon sky,
Or tear-drop welling from old Nature's eye—
A blade of grass, a diamond spray of dew,
But shows thy mystic footsteps sparkling thro'.
Wizard! that forgest thunderbolts at will,
Then peaceful gambol'st down a mountain rill,
Or, leaping from the dark cloud, with a flash,
Level'st whole cities with a deaf'ning crash;
Then turn'st next moment from the low'ring sky

To light a thought in beauty's sparkling eye!
So much that's gentle with thy fierceness blends,
We learn to love thee ere our terror ends.

    Well might the wakening heart of nature thrill,
As Slave of Lamp, obedient to thy will—
When forth, thro' space, careering in mad glee,
Thou spedst full wildly on thy errand free,
And, at thy call, forth from his secret lair
Sprang up the mighty giant men call "Air."
Like molten ore looked forth his glowing eyes,
And hotter still were breathed his burning sighs,
Till the gray mist of space caught up the glow,
And fiery vapor filled the void below.

    O! wondrous sight, a universe all fire!
A cup wherein was brewed each vain desire,
Each grief, each doubt, each love, hate, hope,
    fear, joy,
Each mad ambition and each gilded toy;
Each little appetite, that leads men on,
From doubtless good, till e'en that good is gone;
Each vanity and every virtue, here,
From atoms bubbling, sought their proper sphere,
That each in turn might act their destined part
In their vast theater, the living heart!

For so, from the beginning, went the Word,
When its first whisper fired, and ether stirred.
A mist of fire! the glowing warp and woof
To fashion drapery for Heaven's high roof;
The loom, the universe: the weaver, He
At whose command springs all things—Deity!
He spake and it was done; to Him, all time
Is one eternal NOW—O! thought sublime!
The finite mind shrinks from the task with awe,
When it would measure Him by mortal law.

  Yet ample are His laws. The drop of dew
That hangs a mimic world, proclaims this true;
The rounded tear that falls from childhood's eye,
Is still a globule, like yon orb on high;
The glowing lamp that lights the distant sky,
Or the stray mote that dances in the beam
Of the warm sun, the eddy in the stream—
The desert's grain of sand, the pebble small,
Proclaim the mighty Hand that fashioned all.
From worlds to meaner things, one form gave He,
That man might thence learn meek humility!
Not to despise weak atoms, for from these
Worlds sprang to light, as from small drops spring
      seas!

O! most sublime in their simplicity,
These never-failing laws of Deity.
  Thus, in yon mist of fire, bright spots now gleam,
Like diamond dust they sparkle in the beam
Electric playing o'er them. Nuclei these,
Atomic drops of planetary seas,
Which, true to laws presiding at their birth,
Rotate as surely as the full-grown earth;
And still accumulating as they go,
Collect new forces from the depths below,
Above, around them (everywhere we view
The one pervading principle as true
At work, of like attracting like), till each
Has swelled its bulk to where its limits reach.
  Now may we view each system's early state,
As red-hot liquid masses they rotate
Obedient to a law which science owns,
That fluids meeting in a center, zones
Of quick rotation are established—so
All whirlpools prove, as madly round they go.
And still another law have we to show.
Rotating fluids, drawing as they go
All things attractive, still repel again,
By that same force, all that they can't retain.

And thus each solar system claims its birth,
Formed by the self-same laws man finds on earth
In simplest things; for He who formed them all,
Made the same power by which apples fall
To hold great systems in their proper place,
And keep each courser on the fields of space
From chance encounter in their rapid race!

Seest thou yon monarch of the realms of day,
Whose diadem emits a golden ray,
As thro' morn's opal gates he takes his way?
Why turns the earth, with a glad smile, to greet
His coming, and to kiss his jeweled feet?
Why from each hill-side, meadow, dale, and grove,
Do ringing anthems of melodious love
In matin welcomes rise? O! say, why opes
The flowers' sweet eyes, as lawn and leafy copes
Shake off the glittering dew-drops which the night's
Dark eyes have wept, and hail the dawn's delights?

Does not Dame Nature, with harmonious voice,
Call thro' her mossy dales and groves "Rejoice?"
Bends not the earth in tribute to her sire
Who proudly turns on her his eyes of fire,
Whence spring both warmth and light? O, why,
   say why,

Do all things turn instinctive to the sky,
And rapt adore the Day God's golden sheen,
If ne'er a part of it they once have been?
Is not the voice of nature ever near
To whisper of the parent in child's ear?
And thus, the earth—last youngest-born but two
Of this, our solar household—gives her due
Of reverence meet, her morning greeting fair,
To her crowned sire enthroned in golden air.

For, once, a circling mass of liquid fire,
Our sun filled all our system's space entire;
And gases, metals, earths, all, all were blent
In mass chaotic, thro' space whirling sent.
As ages lapsed, grown colder (as all must
In time), solidifying to a crust,
Its outer edge gave way, as solids will
From fluids part, one law obeying still;
This detached mass, assuming spheral shape,
Rotating in the orbit where escape
From thrall parental first proclaims it free
And eldest born of Sol's vast progeny,
It paces now in never-ending march,
The outer walls of this, our system's arch,
As sentinel, guarding the wide domain,

Where brother soldiers tramp in starry train
Their circling courses, as from parent sun
They sprang to being, as the first had done;
Mars, Jupiter, and Saturn, claiming birth
Of the same sire, their gentle sisters, Earth
And fair-browed Venus honored father call—
And Mercury, the youngest born of all—
Members of the same family, each one,
We find these bright-eyed children of the Sun.

   Go forth, O man, when eve, with glowing cheek
And dewy lip, murmurs a good-night meek,
As in the footsteps of her liege-lord nigh,
She softly follows o'er the faded sky,
Lights the bright taper in her nuptial bower,
Pauses a moment o'er each bridemaid flower
For farewell kiss, then hides her from their sight,
Beneath the envious drapery of night—
Linger, till deep descends still midnight's hour,
List to the voice of Nature, own her power;
Raise but your glances to the arching sky,
Where countless suns and systems ceaseless
   fly— .
Where Sirius sparkles with his diamond blaze,
And Lyra on her golden harp-strings plays,

Arcturus moves resplendent 'mong the stars,
With glowing luster like the shield of Mars—
Bootes with his hounds pursues the Bear,
And Pleiades still mourn—grieved sisters fair,
While Aldebaran's red eye gleams afar,
As Taurus wages ineffectual war
'Gainst bold Orion's sword of golden spheres—
All suns of systems, numbering more years
On Time's hoar chronicle, than mind of man
Can ever grasp within its feeble span
Behold these wonders! then on bended knee
Lift up your humble heart to Deity,
And ask, with prayerful lips, "Lord, what is man,
That thou art mindful of him?" Father, can
So frail a creature claim from thee a thought,
Thou Architect of worlds built out of naught?
Stupendous structures, tangible and bright,
Whose glories from nonentity's dark night,
Forth at thy bidding sprang—thro' ceaseless years
Progressing to these gold illumined spheres,
Teeming with life! And ages yet will show
New worlds and glories, bright'ning as they go,
To swell the wavelets of that stellar sea,
Whose shores are bounded by eternity!

Thus have we seen how solar systems spring,
And from each sun, each planet, once a ring
Detached from the hot mass, condensing still
To a fixed point, its orbit there to fill,
Which, as it cools, may from itself throw off
Its superfluities (tho' skeptics scoff!)
Which, by the laws of nature, fixed as fate,
Around *their* parent mass will then rotate.
Thus satellites are formed, those lesser lights
That with soft silver lamps illume the nights,
When wearied day her western chamber seeks,
And goblin darkness to the owlet speaks—
When bats marauding thro' the dusky air
Rouse the hyena, slumbering in his lair,
And croaking ravens, till the hour has come
For such ill things and elfin shapes to roam.

What Goddess, meek advancing o'er the blue
Etherial pathway of the stars, looks thro'
Their jeweled ranks? An ornate silver shield,
Upon a diamond-studded azure field,
Is her insignia! 'Tis bright Luna, she
In fable, Goddess of fair Chastity—
But whom men know as gentle Ladye Moon,
She comes to smile away "night's cheerless noon!"

Earth's fair-browed daughter she, her only one—
Thrown from that earth, as earth from parent sun,
And ever lending to her mother dear
A smile of love, her gloomy night to cheer.
If then, each mighty orb that lights the blue
Empyrean, has sprung to being, true
To laws presiding o'er the whole, and all
From matter in one vast stupendous ball—
May we not also judge, that all contain
Constituent elements, which lose or gain
A density, as subject more or less
To those controlling causes which compress,
Expand, solidify, evaporize
All gases, metals, known beneath the skies?
The chemist tells of certain substances
Called Elements, and by combining these,
All forms of matter in and round our earth,
Are represented in primordial birth—
As water, from two gases mingling, springs,
The liquid compound of these vaporous things;
The metal silicium, in *quantum suf.*,
With oxygen unites to form the rough
Silica, base of nearly half the rocks;
While carbon sparkles in the ebon blocks,

The massive walls, and wide-spread, jetty domes,
Where the poor miners make their dismal homes,
As well as in the diamond's sparkling rays
Which in a monarch's jeweled scepter blaze;
And nitrogen, of which our atmosphere
Is four-fifths formed, among them doth appear;
While different metals with a gas combined,
In magnesia, alumin, lime, we find.
Yet solids, liquids, fluids æriform,
Are all reducible to simple form
Which elementary we call; of these
Are gases, six; metallic substances,
In number forty-two; the rest not classed,
But which, as elements, must not be passed,
For carbon stands within the group, a small
Ingredient in the atmosphere, but all
Of animal or vegetable kind
Are with its subtle essence intertwined,
The base on which they rest; and fossils, too,
Formed from the latter, it impregnates thro';
As coal will show, within whose dusky bed
Masses of carbon are deposited.
    If these constituent elements that all
Of matter else is formed from, on this ball,

Have sprung themselves from primordial form
Of matter, which some fierce, organic storm,
Obeying certain laws, has caused produce,
Analogy would teach us to deduce,
The same conditions liable to take place,
In all the regions of infinite space,
As are the laws of centrifugal force
Or gravitation ; and, if so, of course
The gases, metals, earths, exist as true
(Conditions being proper), where the blue,
Unbroken ether fans the golden light
Of astral systems, glorious and bright,
Yet far remote, beyond the span of mind
To fathom, as the wanderings of the wind
"That bloweth where it listeth," as on earth,
Where science metes to them this glorious birth.
    Matter, if springing then from but one cause,
Or many more (as may be), under laws
That differ in effects, shows varied forms ;
As cold condenses ; heat, expanding, warms.
Put water under arctic temperature,
And solid barriers guard the ice-bound shore ;
Place the same liquid in the boiler red
With heat, and wreathing, curling overhead,

The vapor moist in graceful folds ascends,
Expanding, as with air it freely blends,
Filling more space than when a liquid mass,
Or by cold hardened to a wall of glass.

Thus heat, we find's a powerful agent here
In regulating matter in our sphere.
And science tells us how much added heat
Would be required, to 'vaporize complete,
The waters of our globe—and how much more,
To free the solids of their gaseous store,
And with increasing temperature, to bring
The whole to vapor, whence it first did spring.

'Tis then, existing temperature, which lends
The earth its present volume, and which blend
The elements in compound form, and gives
Conditions whereby man and creature lives.
And chilling off with age, is nature's law—
For that the earth has colder grown, no flaw
We find in research ever to exist,
In refutation of the fact. The mist
Of fire, wherein each solar system formed,
Agglomerated, till its surface swarmed
With eddying circles, cooling as they turned,
Till each a mighty sun in splendor burned,

Which cooling still, threw off its planet host—
The first of which, escaped, of course, could boast
More heat than could the next—and so, till all
Were whirling sent from the great golden ball,
Which still retained warmth-giving power and light
Enough to dissipate each planet's night.

Take our own system—view each planet there—
Their densities form argument most fair
In favor of the theory; for earth
Claiming o'er Mercury and Venus, birth
Antecedent, hath matter more diffuse
Than either; which will force us to deduce
That 'twas because the earth was formed when heat
Was greater in our system; so complete
Throughout that system's range, this unity
Among its planetic community,
Is marked. Mars, Jupiter, and Saturn, still
Are lighter, as in circling turns, they fill
Respective limits in our system's space.
And Herschel, elder still in planet race,
In his diffusive matter, shows that heat
Preponderated, when his glowing feet
First trod the azure. And, may it not be
So ordered, that these distant worlds shall see

Less of the sun's light, feel less of his heat,
Because their *inward* warmth makes all complete!
While those that's nearest to the fountain-head
(As Mercury, for instance, dense as lead)
Exist beneath an atmosphere of cold,
Which call for solar rays of heat fourfold,
To make them habitable.

                    Wise, those laws,
By Him ordained, the great All-giving Cause!—
Who hath attempered every dwelling-place
In His wide empire, to each varied race
That He hath placed there. For, no cause have we
To doubt existence on those orbs we see
Obeying laws, which govern earth as well,
Where sentient beings are well-known to dwell.
No right have we—presuming as we are—
To dare deny to one pale, trembling star
That sails with earth our system's waveless sea,
Its birthright's due, its being's destiny!
As theaters of life, young nurseries
For budding virtues, and rich argosies
Of dawning hopes and aspirations high
That reach beyond the blue, o'erarching sky,
Are those bright orbs that ever ceaseless fly!

Or crucibles where every grain of good
Is filtered from its dross, to be the food
Of angels, in those higher realms where man
Will walk transparent, when his little span
Of life is past, and mind shall have progressed
Beyond its clayey covering—then the rest
Shall be as noon-day clear—as on, still on
Thro' Heaven's bright aisles, until the goal is won,
And God revealed, in majesty sublime,
Great Self-existent Founder of all time!—
Shines o'er his works brighter than midday sun,
And gives his creature welcome—with "Well done,
Thou good and faithful servant, enter thou
Into the joys prepared for thee!"
                                        And now
(These facts admitted), it is clearly shown,
Our globe's a specimen of all the known,
And similarly placed orbs, that run
Their circling courses round our common sun—
That is, as far as matter, and the laws
Which govern it are known—with but this clause:
That varied shades will from conditions spring—
And bodies *here* that's solid, *there* may wing
In vapory folds, or in soft liquid flow,

As inner heat sends forth expanding glow.
If then, we're "one of many," let us seek
With earnest faith, and reverence true and meek,
To gain a knowledge of our mother earth,
Since we have seen there's nothing in her birth
That differs from all other planets known.
In her, we then, have but a sample shown
Of myriad orbs, that—like the desert's sand
Whose grains are numberless—on every hand,
Above, around us circle !

      Let us look
In Nature's ever open " story-book,"
And read upon its pages, truths sublime,
There traced by never-erring " Father Time."
Quaint chronicles on every leaf marks he—
Sometimes upon the margin, " Destiny "—
But still, the running title clear and bright,
We'll find o'er all, lettered both full and light—
" Progression !"—Earth's brown cover lift and see
Its footsteps over mountain, rock, and lea !

The Earth.

THE wondrous Earth! diversified with vales
And mounts, rocks, forests, rivers, meadows, dales,
Blue, dimpling lakes and foaming oceans deep—
White, towering glaciers—dark ravines and steep
Acclivities—fierce torrents, rushing free
O'er jutting crags, to form a raging sea
Of surge—and tiny rivulets that sing
A cheerful song, as onward still they wing
Their modest way to the great deep—all, all
That's beauteous, grand, terrific, on this ball—
That wakes our wonder, or calls forth our praise,
Or startles, even while we raptured gaze—
Must still inspire more wonder, reverence, awe,
When, as results of an unchanging law
We view them!—And this proof of it we'll bring—
'Tis from conditions meeting, all things spring,
In manner called spontaneous—each thing

Inanimate, and those with life endowed!—
Tho' mystery the manner may enshroud
To our dull visions; yet effects we see,
Showing us, that 't is from spontaneity
All changes geological take place
Upon the earth, and, also, that each race
Of animals, from meaner things that crawl,
To man, by each acknowledged lord of all
Terrestrial things, have in like manner been
Produced.   Spontaneous the action, seen
Thro' its effects; and electricity's
The powerful agent to accomplish these
(To us) most wonderful results—divine
In origin, omnipotent, sublime!
     'T is thus, the great, all-wise Creator shows
His majesty!   O! think not that it throws
One tittle of contempt upon his power
To show, that by fixed laws—a godly dower—
He works his ever comprehensive will:
It proves the mighty mind, more mighty still,
That has the power to frame harmonious laws,
Progressive thro' all time, from simplest cause
To most sublime effect, than to affirm
That Deity, *in person*, placed each germ,

To wave in foliage o'er each circling sphere,
Where first it sprang to being! O! no fear
That reasoning minds to this delusion long
Shall yield, when truthful Nature, with her throng
Of witnesses, attests the glorious power
That's worked Time's lever from its starting hour,
That's calling, now, new wonders from the mist
In which—like fire in the volcano's heart—exist
The subtile elements, with impulse rife,
Waiting the touch of some organic strife
To reproduce them in their outward form,
As the red thunderbolt is born of storm!

    All elemental substances are found
United in some compound form. Thus, round
Our globe aerial draperies curl,
As oxygen and nitrogen unfurl
Their gaseous banners, waved in union, where
Their folds uniting, form our atmosphere!
But tho' thus blent in vapory union,
They're never found alone in nature; one,
Of water's a third part; and in each kind
Of rock in the earth's crust, we also find
This gas abundant—while the other claims
The "better-half" of Air's wide-spread domains,

And freely blends with many simple things,
If but attraction waves inviting wings—
For, there are predilections strange, in these
Aeriform, metallic substances,
Toward each other's company. We find
(So says the chemist) two of these combined
In a solution; add a third, and see
One of the former to the latter flee—
Then introduce a fourth, the third will leave,
The first and firmly to the stranger. cleave!

   Few rocks there are in which can not be found,
Two forms of matter, each of which abound
In elementary substances combined—
While in the diamond, carbon pure we find,
Alone; thus showing, combinations and
Recombinations blend on every hand;
Conditions meet conditions, and thence spring
All forms of matter, and each living thing!
For such are but earth's majestatic laws—
There's no effect but there exists a cause.

   Now that our globe was in a fluid state
When finally solidifying, great
Existing proof have we; the very form
Which a revolving body, soft and warm,

Will always take from centrifugal force,
Our earth possesses, which departs, of course,
Just so much from a perfect sphere, as shows
The workings of that inner law, which throws
Preponderance toward the equatorial zone,
Where earth's diameter exceeds, 'tis known,
Its polar depth, and proves our planet's form
To be an oblate spheroid; not warm
(As once) upon its outer crust, but deep
In its huge subterranean chambers sleep
The smoldering fires—a residuum
Of that great heat which kept vaporiform
All matter in times past—and whence arise
Volcanoes flaming, towering to the skies!

The lamp of science throws its piercing ray
Thro' earth's green coverlet and wild rocks gray,
And by its light, shining distinct and clear,
The beauteous law of Order doth appear
In the arrangements of the solid crust,
Whose basis rock of crystalline, 't is just
To infer, must rest upon the fused mass
Of matter in earth's center—thence we pass
To layer, or strata, which from water seems
To 've been deposited; but this, by streams

Of melted rock volcanically sent
From the chaotic mass below, is rent
In fissures; and again, are chinks,
Where veins of many metals lay—broad links
Of yellow gold, pale silver, duller lead,
And red-eyed iron are deposited,
Thus forming, at first sight, a most confused,
Disordered scene.   But when we have perused
The leaves of the "stone book," we will have
      hived
Instruction only from such source derived;
A knowledge of the history of our globe,
The which to gain, we must its vitals probe.
  The deposition of the aqueous rocks,
And the projection of volcanic blocks,
Have taken place since Earth its present form's
Assumed.   And still take place, as the wild storms
Of Ætna and Vesuvius plainly show;
Where the red lava's seething, molten flow
(The rocky scum of each fused element
O'er-boiling the huge caldrons where they're
      blent),
Rains liquid fire upon the plains around,
Which cooling, solid rock is always found.

And the deep sea, in never-ceasing flow,
Her stores of sediment still leaves below;
And as fresh layers upon her rocky bed
She freely scatters, thro' the mass is spread
Diffusive heat from the great fires beneath,
And from its action, thus, another sheath
Or coating's added to the basis rock
Of earth's broad wall of crystal, block on block.
And so, old Earth is ever filling up
Her inequalities—for where the cup
Of mighty seas sunk deep within her breast
(Deeper than those which now within it rest),
Granitic mountains reared their scraggy heads
From ocean's ever restless, surging beds,
And tireless waves still chafed the rocky sides,
Bearing the granules on their flowing tides,
Which "constant dripping" will wear off—to fill
The cavities below. And this is still
The means used now, as in times formerly,
To give the earth a smooth rotundity.
  'T is science tells us that the seas of old
Were deeper far by many, many fold,
Than now; and this is by the primary rocks
Well proved, of which, the lofty, towering blocks;

4

That guard old Scotia's burns and flow'ry braes
Are fine examples. These, formed in those
    days
Of eld, the earliest stratified, and first
Series that from earth's crystal bosom burst,
Are called the *gneiss system and mica slate.*
The thickness of these beds is oft so great
That it attests the mighty depths profound
Of the primeval oceans that around,
(Perhaps) above them circled.

                    Now, these rocks,
These early stratified, primeval blocks,
Bear witness of a higher temperature,
A stronger heat than any, we are sure,
Within earth's crust; nor one of them contains
A vestige of the petrified remains
Of vegetation or of creature—found
In other rocks so freely to abound
To tell a wondrous tale of times long past—
And from their absence in a field so vast
As these present, we must infer that none
Existed; that the earth displayed but one
Vast face of ponderous rock or boiling sea,
Where naught of verdure, flower, or shrub, or tree,

Waved its soft foliage on the sterile air,
Nor animal crouched in his covert lair,
Nor fish in the hot waves disporting, laved,
Nor wing of bird the heated ether cleaved;
But silence, broken only by the roar
Of the wild waters dashing on the shore,
Hung o'er the lonely scene !
                The march toward life
Had not commenced as yet. Organic strife
In never-ceasing changes, still evoked
Conditions new, to part the chain which yoked
Existence in its rocky prison deep,
And loose that element from pristine sleep,
Which clothes the forest in its mantle green,
And o'er earth's bosom folds an emerald screen;
From which each blade of grass, each sheaf of
    grain,
Sucks in the principles which life sustain !
  And what this substance? Carbon—known to be
Of herb and plant the main commodity—
From them to animals, by transit rare
'Tis passed, and back again restored to air
In each expired breath the latter sends—
So that with all things, thus 't is shown, it blends

The great life-giving principle ! and found
In the next strata freely to abound
In beds of limestone; and 't is there are shown
The first remains of living creatures known :
The forms of *zoophites, polypes*
(Those tireless builders in the restless seas
Where coral palaces attest their skill,
Their perseverance, industry, and will !)
And *mollusks*—these, the fossils which betray
The life-productions of that early day,
Of which the species now are swept away;
For 't is resemblance, only, that they show
In general character, to those below
Old ocean's briny billows, where they lave
To-day, the portals of the sea-king's cave.
And with them, various sea-plants, also sprung
Spontaneous in their watery beds, and clung
The first link in the chain of nutriment.
And so, by links, all forms of life are blent!
Conditions are advanced—and one by one,
A higher order is produced. 'T is shown,
That in the eras of those early rocks,
A tropic clime prevailed; and as the blocks
Of other series reared their stately heads,

From the retreating ocean's watery beds,
A cooler temperature still wrought more change;
And varied petrifactions in each range,
Give, in quaint characters, on stony page
(*If man would only heed*), their lessons sage!
Thus in the *Old Red Sandstone* fish abound,
That nowhere in earth's waters now are found;
Nor only in one section of our sphere,
In those old rocks, do these remains appear.
In lands antipodal, where'er is found,
The strata of that system, types abound
Of uniform condition—which doth show
This form of life organic, in its flow,
Was coeval with those primeval rocks;
And not until the *Secondary* blocks,
Or ranges *Carboniferous*, was seen,
Upon the earth's broad bosom, aught of green
Luxuriance or verdure; no land plant,
Or animal remains, ere these, extant,
To prove that such existed.

Thence, 't is clear,
The mighty mandate, " Let dry land appear,"
Was by earth's majestatic laws obeyed
(The produce of conditions all arrayed

In favorable progress), at the close
Of the first strata.   Then volcanic throes,
In nature's bosom spoke the mighty birth,
Of the great mountain ranges of our earth.
Dry land was formed, and vegetation reared
Its head spontaneous—towering shrubs appeared,
Of which no species now on earth are known;
Because the temperature, 't is clearly shown,
Too cold is for existing types to be
Developed to such size.   And thus, we see,
The forests of those days abundant spread
(As their deposits in each dusk coal-bed
Must plainly prove—geology doth show
Hundreds of species in this strata low).
The fern or bracken then in lofty trees,
Waved in wild foliage on each tropic breeze,
Sweeping o'er earth's warm breast in music sweet,
Where now the Ice-king stalks with freezing feet;
But still no flowering shrub or luscious fruit
Spread tempting banquet round for bee or brute—
No hum of bird or insect's waving wings,
Nor higher types of animated things
Shone o'er the scene.   And from this, it would seem
That this luxuriant vegetable stream,

Was but designed the atmosphere to free
Of matter noxious to organic life—and be
A means, as well, to lay up mineral store
To benefit the *human* tides, which pour
Their floods from North, South, East, and West,
    to-day,
And to Omniscient Source their tribute pay!
  We pass from these to other rocks, and here
We find new marvels. On our startled ear
Breaks a low whisper from our mother, Earth:
"Behold! the forms to which was given birth
Spontaneous—in creatures made to be
Dwellers alike of either land or sea!"
Yes, in these rocks are found the fossil forms
Of reptiles huge; and, also, mammoth swarms
Of creatures now unknown, but still allied
To crocodiles and lizards—and beside,
Are numerous tortoises of monstrous growth;
And all these creatures blend the types of
    both
Land animals and fish—that is, they live
In water, yet can breathe the air—and give
In one (*the rynchosaurus*), beak and feet
Of bird, and reptile body—to complete

The link between these two. So Nature blends
Each changing type as higher she ascends !
　And thus, the *New Red Sandstone* era shows
Commencement of *Reptilia*, and throws
Advancing steps toward the next order—birds.
Then the succeeding series, formed two-thirds
Of *Oolite* (a limestone in round grains
Like to a fish's roe), give the remains
Of reptiles still, and insects ; also, here,
The first marks of *Mammalia* appear—
The fossil of a quadruped, as clear
To prove the progress that the busy earth
Had made in creatures of spontaneous birth—
For by this petrifaction, we infer
The lowest order of this mammifer,
Marsupialia—here first was seen—
And still new plants ; which prove the clime
　　t' have been
A tropical and temperate between.
Thus showing, still decreasing temperature,
And new advancing types appearing here,
The while the old in gradual decay,
Were from their scene of being swept away.
　The next formed rocks cretaceous are. Of these,

The white cliffs of Old England, o'er the seas,
That stretch broad arms to shield their native land
From depredation—guardians of the strand!—
Are specimens.   In such chalk-beds are seen
Great hollows, with clay, limestone, marl between—
And these mixed beds (which have divided been
Into three classes), show new species, still,
Of animals—thus, link by link, to fill
The gap between the earliest formed and man,
According to earth's grand organic plan
By infinite intelligence arranged !
Which mortal arrogance has never changed,
Tho' fanatics have wordy thunders hurl'd
Above a strangely self-deluded world,
To prove their Maker in his laws did err,
Which failed to fashion man.
                              We must infer,
From petrifactions in this strata found,
That earth had reached, in her progressive round,
The period whose glimmering dawn would rise
To noonday splendor; when the arching skies
Would wave bright banners o'er the bounteous
        lands,
That, still obeying the Divine commands,

5

Would bring forth living creature, creeping thing,
And every feathered warbler that doth wing
Its way thro' the blue ether; when great whales
Would part the billows, and the finny sails
Gliding o'er oceans' watery mirrors blue,
Would still proclaim their laws of being true—
Fulfilling the great mandate which went forth
In the beginning, and thus prove its worth
In earth's increasing fruitfulness!

                                       Begin
With the first period of this era.   In
Its shell deposits, vast remains are found,
Showing *mammalia* freely to abound,
Of higher types—*Pachydermata*.   These
Are long extinct in direct species,
But still approximating to that class
That now on earth crops the luxuriant grass.
And others still, allied to wolf and fox,
Opossum, raccoon, squirrel—in these blocks
Of *Tertiary Formation*.   Species, too,
Of birds allied to sea-lark, quail, curlew
And buzzard, owl and pelican, and new
Forms of reptiles.   Then the next periods give
Advancing types of creatures vast that live

'Neath the wave: marine mammalia, here,
Seals, dolphins, whales, walruses now appear;
And still progressing, on the land are shown
The mastodon and mammoth, now unknown,
With other animals gigantic, prone
To exist in times gone by, as if the earth
Used a refining process in each birth,
And modeled and remodeled every type,
That each incongruous feature she might wipe
From the progressive being, till it shone
The prototype of the Almighty One,
Whose wondrous word, "In our own image, man
Shall fashioned be!" went forth when time began.
    From these huge creatures—which the elephant
Is now the existing species of—we want
New orders; and behold! we find them here
In *Ruminantia*—as camels, deer,
And oxen, now, for the first time appear,
And these, with other ruminants, but fill
The points progressive to *Bimana*. Still,
A gap is left in the ascending scale,
And lo! what fills it? Surely we don't fail,
In pointing to the *Quadrumana?* There
The link, that must resolve all doubts to air!

Showing the blended types of man and beast,
And with intelligence enough at least
To cause us wonder if the (so-called) brute,
Is destitute of reason, altho' mute?
  'T is to Geology we owe the light
That dissipates the darkness of the night,
Brooding above the labyrinthine past,
And read its history by the gleam so cast.
A never-ending volume, always new,
With fresh leaves placed by time while journeying
      thro',
And to its bulk will each succeeding age,
Still add a wonderful, transcendent page!
From low volcanic depths to mountain heights,
Time's restless pencil still this axiom writes:
Spontaneous formation of each thing!
From zephyr floating by on viewless wing,
To raging winds that toss the mighty seas;
From the young leaf that trembles on the breeze,
To the gnarled oak that braves the storm-king's
      wrath;
In every grain of sand, in every path
That chafing oceans mark upon the rocks;
In every varied tribe of feathered flocks,

That part the azure curtains of the air;
In each fierce creature crouching in his lair;
And e'en in lordly man, we read this truth,
Self-evident to all from age to youth—
That each inanimate and living thing
Must from spontaneous action ever spring!
Note the firm earth, its far-spread, ranging blocks
Of massive, ponderous and towering rocks—
Of what composed? Of water crystallized,
Solidified—and all, evaporized
May be by heat. For, water but appears,
The well-known produce of two blended airs
By electricity combined. And this,
The fluid, that our solid planet is
Composed of; it surrounds the globe in mists,
And deep within the crust of earth exists
In springs—deeper, appears a sea, as shown
By wells artesian, which to all are known—
Deeper, it is conjectured to exist,
A sea of condensed steam, or scalding mist—
And deeper still, in mass chaotic lies,
From whose hot, molten bed volcanoes rise.
    And thus around us, do we see effects
Of spontaneity, for who rejects

The theory, that conditions must be right,
To work such wondrous changes, which our sight
Convinces us have taken place within
Our globe?   These facts to prove, we must begin
At the beginning, thence, progressive rise
Upon the chain whose end is in the skies!
    Nothing was e'er created to be lost.
The waif, on ocean's billow tempest-tost,
Hath still its mission, trifling tho' it be—
And what but *drops* is every mighty sea?
And atoms infinite, form rolling spheres,
Succeeding moments swell to hoary years—
And all are marching toward the dawning light
That parts the curtains of the dying night,
And lets the day-beam splendor in, to show
To man benighted, all the heavenly glow
Which God's grand laws progressing, shed around
O'er earth and skies, where'er effects are found!
There's nothing insubstantial—the breath
Of air we breathe, on which hangs life and death,
Can be by pressure turned to fluid form,
The fleeting rainbow hues that ride the storm,
Are prisoned in the diamond's crystal cell—
The thoughts engendered in man's brain, can swell

To outward shape in " words that burn," and leave
Their mark on memory's brow to joy or grieve,
Thrill with enthusiasm or depress with fear
As now they burst, now sink upon the ear.
Even shadow, held of all terrestrial things
Most fleeting—the daguerreotypist brings
Within the range of certain laws, and see
The shadow's fixed by spontaneity!

And thus, the changing forms of Earth have
been
Produced. Thro' each succeeding era seen
Developed to superior orders still—
Each range of rocks the circle vast to fill;
And these again volcanically rent,
With matter new, projected thro' each vent,
Which new conditions still evoke effects,
And counter-causes all the old rejects—
Sweeping away successive races still,
Which have played out the part they were to
fill ;
Progressive steps, toward a completed whole,
Which under laws eternal ceaseless roll!
For all must know, the lofty pines that rise
In grandeur towering to the bending skies,

Sprang from the simple cone in earth's dark bed,
As tender saplings first, ere overhead
Their green plumes wave where eagles proudly
    soar—
And animals and worlds can do no more—
For *all* from germs to forms complete progress,
'T is nature's law, 'gainst which there 's no redress !

    Each discord has its harmony, each storm
Its calm, each light its shade, and every form
Of pain its pleasure, every throb its rest,
Each aim its object ; and tho' last, still best
We find on earth that each thing has its place,
In the triumphal march, the mighty race
From inanition to intelligence ;
And still progressing upward, onward, thence
To immortality—when faith shall rise
Exultant o'er the grave to glorious skies !

    We find in nature, certain substances
That form connecting ties, which by degrees,
From matter lead to life ; thence, link by link,
From lowest form that trembles on the brink
Of being, up to man.   As bitumen
And sulphur are the links the earth between
And metals ; vitriols, metals join, 't is known,

With salts; crystallizations, salts with stone;
The amianthis and cytophites
Most surely form a certain species
Of tie 'twixt stones and plants; the polypus
'Tween plants and insects; and the tube-worm,
    thus
Leads off to shells and reptiles; then, the eel
And water-serpent, also, seem to steal
A path from reptiles on to fish; a medium
'Tween fish and birds, the anas nigra come;
The bat and flying-squirrel still link birds
To quadrupeds; and so, the chattering herds
Of monkeys, are the band 'twixt beast and man.
A chain of beings on progressive plan.
  We see effects of natural law, where'er
We turn our eyes upon the rolling sphere;
Effects, from which we *must* this fact deduce:
That 't is conditions proper which produce
Each change of verdure and organic life!
One step beyond a previous order, rife.
With principles progressive, ever gives
Advancing types of everything that lives,
Or being has, upon prolific Earth.
And thus it is, the individual birth

Of a new form of verdure, sprang from change
In the conditions since the previous range,
Thus differing the effects. We also see,
Spontaneous growth of flower, bush, shrub, or
    tree,
In this wise: When salt-springs upon the land
Break out far from the sea, on every hand
Do salt or seaside plants spring up, tho' none
Grew there before. And this is only one
Example. Mold from vast depths thrown, we
    know,
Exposed to atmospheric action, so
Becomes spontaneously verdure clad
With plants that there no previous being had.
When lakes are drained new vegetation springs.
And among other proved spontaneous things,
'Tis told, when London was laid low by fire,
The surface of the ruined part, entire,
Became completely covered with the plant
Sisymbrium irio! And there are extant
Innumerable instances' to show
Spontaneous production here below.
    Nor only vegation thus induced—
Organic life is by like means produced.

The mites we see in cheese spontaneous spring;
And close-kept furs their stock of moths will
　　bring,
As foul-kept hedges generate the slug.
These actions all admit, who do not hug
Delusion as their guide, and still deny
Existence, but as work of Deity
In *propria persona*, nor pause
To ask themselves, why universal laws
In one department of creation may
Not work as well as in another? Say
Does it not elevate our Maker more,
That by these laws, mysterious, slow and sure,
And *never-failing*, all things are produced?
Than to suppose him (mortal-like) reduced
To *fashion with his hands* the model, whence
Each prototype (*by different process*) thence
Was ever after to be made? Weak, weak,
The causality that thus would seek
To blind itself, and bring Divinity
To human standard!
　　　　　　　All these orbs we see
Rolling thro' space, have in like way progressed
From comprehensive germ, which all the rest

Of future grand development evolved.
This is self-evident.   Yet man—resolved
In bold defiance of known nature's laws,
And even while admitting a First Cause—
Asserts a *direct act* of Divine power
Which placed *him* here, to live his little hour,
A trifle longer than the ephemera!
The God of many worlds! by whose wise law
Great systems circle—forced to interfere
With His established laws to usher here,
Weak man upon the theater of his
Existence!   O, if Atheism is
Extant, 'tis in a creed like this, which gives
To God a limit!

                        Ah! there surely lives
Not a reflective mind but sees how far
Above all mortal power God's workings are!
His workings, thro' eternities unchanged,
Thro' *all* departments of creation ranged
On principles which human skill defy
To alter, for their superstructures lie
On one firm basis—Order! which is known,
To be in nature the great corner-stone,
On which is reared the towering fanes where swell

The pæans grand, their Author's praise to tell!
The arching skies that roof cathedrals vast,
Ionic columned in Time's quarry cast,
And hung with pictures which a Claude Lorraine,
Might ceaseless strive to imitate in vain;
Where every whispering breeze and waving leaf,
Conveys a moral or a sermon brief;
Where feathered choristers harmonious raise,
Their untaught anthems of melodious praise,
And incense rising from the flowers, floats thro'
The ivied portals wet with morning dew;
And Man, the High Priest, at the altar stands,
Confirmed as such by God's most holy hands!
Who gives to him dominion o'er the earth,
And every living thing that there claims birth;
Fish in the seas, and fowls that cleave the air,
Cattle, and creeping thing that moveth there—
All these in man their master still must find,
And bow before the majesty of mind!
Yea, mind! the light planned by Divinity,
To be developed when the clay should be
Progressed upon the earth thro' ever still
Succeeding species upward, higher, till
The full-formed being shone with godlike brow,

Its Maker's image, to which all things bow!
That by this all-controlling principle
Of mind, should be almost invincible,
And fitted for a future glorious race,
Of immortality and endless grace.

    Away with superstition, whine, and cant!
For sound reflection's all we ever want
To teach us mighty truths. An eye to see,
A heart to feel the works of Deity!
A mind unprejudiced by bigotry—
A soul from all sectarianism free,
That gives God praise for all that round us lies,
And makes him Lord of earth, and seas, and
    skies!
Progenitor of laws progressing still,
Thro' whole eternities to work his will,
In minute steps, which fall, as falls the sand
To mark the hours—around on every hand,
Till from the atom mighty worlds round out,
And new conditions ever bring about
Their changes, till those rolling worlds have given
In man, the link between all earths and Heaven!

    And thus, the morning stars shall sing for joy!
Each planet praises ring without alloy,

When to that point progressed which ushers man
Upon his scene of being—which began
O'er earth to dawn as closed the era known
As that of *Tertiary Formations*, shown
To contain the traces of existence still
Of higher types, the ascending scale to fill.
And we have seen that each successive race
Was swept away, yet leaving still a trace
To mark that once they lived.   Research doth
        show
In that remote, far distant " long ago,"
That five distinct, successive races vast,
Of plants existed, now gulfed in the past;
And four distinct, successive races more,
Of animals, lived in those days of yore,
Before the present race, with man, appeared.

    How many countless ages may have reared
Their cycles o'er the rolling earth the while,
We know not.   When we view each ponderous pile
Of mineral productions—each coal-bed
Whose fossil masses o'er vast areas spread;
And think what time's required to vegetate,
And to produce the carbon, which in great
Quantities, all coal-fields generate;

Or cast our glances o'er the towering blocks
Of solid stratified, or aqueous rocks
Which old retreating oceans have laid bare,
And think by what slow process, layer on layer,
Their present bulk's attained; or turn our eyes
To where the fierce volcanic fires arise
From Hecla's regions of perpetual snow—
See Etna's hissing, surging, molten flow
Of lava—and Vesuvius, Stromboli,
And numbers in the isles of the South Sea—
In Asia, Africa, America,
Where'er these furnaces projected are—
And then reflect, no human records show
The moment when these fires began to glow
(With but a few exceptions) in each mount,
That from time immemorial's been the fount
Whose seething jets fall in a golden rain
To make another Danaë of each plain!
And that each mountain range that girts our earth,
Owes to such inward struggle still its birth—
And all by slow, progressive steps, 't is seen,
Developed to their present state have been—
The mind shrinks back, and fails to grasp the sum
Of multiplying units as they come

To give the age of Earth!

                        Man's life's a rill

Beside creation's gulf—a fraction still

Of a compounded whole—a drop within

Time's ever rolling ocean circling—

A second on the dial's endless round—

A mote in Nature's golden sunbeam found—

A tiny mountain stream by torrent free,

But flowing on to swell the tidal sea

Of Progress! Such the destiny of man,

And worlds, and systems, since Time's march began.

   6

Man.

WE now must solve the mighty problem, Man!
Roll back the curtain, Faith! that we may scan
His attributes—and thou, O mother Earth!
Turn to the page whereon we read his birth
Recorded in Old Time's Biography—
Tho' entered there in quaint stenography,
'Tis to the eye of Reason, lettered clear!
 Now, " Open Sesame." What see we here?
A point where ceaseless progress has evolved
Conditions new, and Nature has resolved
To test her powers, a higher race to give
In her ancestral palaces to live.
We've seen her handiwork, her curious chain
Of plants and animals, progress amain,
From sea-weeds to land plants, the simplest, first,
Ere to fruition the more complex burst—
Her life organic, in the humble forms
Of zoophytes, radiata, swarms

(66)

Of mollusca, articulata, ere
A higher order shone upon our sphere;
Then fishes, reptiles, birds, mammalia
(First of which is marsupialia,
The lowest forms of mammifers) are seen,
Each a progressive step from what has been,
And giving earnest, still, of what may be
Developed yet, thro' all eternity!
And showing how all forms are bound in one
Upon our globe—a mighty chain, begun
'Mongst lowliest mosses, onward, link by link,
Binding organic things, till on the brink
Of immortality, it circles man,
Last of created things, whose mortal span
Of life being o'er, shall then triumphant rise
To his new form of being in the skies!

    The physiologist observes, each animal
Progresses still, while in the germinal,
Thro' changes, all resembling the forms
Of lower orders in the scale. The worms,
Being lowest of articulata—see,
An insect at the order's héad, will be
In larva state, an annelid, or worm;
And thus, with every embryo, or germ.

The frog is first a fish with gills, to fit
It for aquatic life—and still, as it
Advances to maturity, a change
In its formation, then admits its range
Upon the land.   And higher classes still
Of mammifers, the fixed forms must fill
In embryo, of orders in the scale
Beneath them.   Even mighty man don't fail
In this fulfillment of the law—'t is shown,
His organization passes thro' all known
Conditions, in the germinal, and gives
(In resemblance only) type of each that lives
The permanent established form, below
Him, of the various orders as they go
Advancing upward.   His first form is shown
That, which in *animalculæ* is known
To be fixed; his brain will then assume
The form of a true fish's; then 't will loom
The more distinct brain of a reptile; still
In transitu, a bird's, a rodent's, will
The type be; then, that of a ruminant—
Digitigrada's the next type we want,
And lo! the fœtal brain evolves it now;
Then the next change, and nearly last, will show

The characteristics of the perfect ape ;
This when supprest, there seems to be a gap
In the ascending scale—'t is then, that man,
Formed from each creature's best, by Wisdom's
    plan,
The human type assumes.   That is, the brain
Is then complete, the last link in the chain
Of earthly things, that *yet* have been exhumed
From the prolific dust of ages ! tombed
In whose vast mausoleum mighty.Truth
Has dormant lain thro' the world's thoughtless
    youth ;
But Reason's trump, like Gabriel's blast, shall wake
The dead—the tower of Superstition shake,
Until its weakened portals crumbling fall,
And grandly o'er the charred and somber pall
Of blackened ashes, buried Truth shall rise,
A phœnix soaring in effulgent skies !
    That man 's an animal, his attributes
Must plainly prove, and silence all disputes.
Considered zoologically, he
The type above all others, seems to be ;
The head of animated nature here.
And as, in every order on our sphere

Are different species existing found,
So, in *Bimana*, differing types abound,
From lower ranging to the higher still,
The order's circle thus complete to fill.
We 'll give each species, as 't is shown their birth
Successively took place upon the earth,
Where climate and conditions governed each
Advance, as all effects full surely teach
   The first, then, of the genus *homo* (shown
By all analogy in nature known,
To be *spontaneously produced*), appeared
When atmospheres caloric far upreared
A torrid climate o'er the rolling earth,
Too hot for other forms of human birth
Than that, by constitution, color, seen
Adapted to withstand the heat, has been,
And still is, *relatively* speaking, shown
To be confined to torrid climes—the known,
Thick-lipped, flat-nosed, and frizzled, woolly-haired
Inhabitant of Africa.   Compared
With other known conditions of mankind,
This species, in their barbarism, blind
Superstitions, and loose morals, and in
Their intellectual desolation (twin

Children of one parent), their features coarse,
Their dark, ungainly forms, and voices hoarse—
In all these, differ, more than do the rest
From that type known to be the last and best—
The Indo-European or Caucasian race.
(Our own impartial Jefferson did trace
Between the Black and White man, many points
Of difference.   He says : The Black anoints
His body more profusely than the White
With perspiration; and there is a slight
Difference in the arrangement of the mass
Of lungs, by which, 't is clear, the Black can pass
His breath with greater force than the White man ;
Less beard he has his mouth's broad arch to span ;
And in the shape of body, color, hair,
They differ ; while the Negro's needful share
Of sleep requires to be less than the White's ;
The ardor of his love display invites,
But deals less in imagination than
That of the more idealistic man,
Whose finer organization leads to less
Of animal preponderance and excess.
The Black is more adventurous, while his grief
More transient is, and quicker finds relief ;

Less he reflects; his reasoning powers are
Decidedly inferior; by far
His mind's best feature, memory,
Which, equal to the White's is known to be;
But not imagination: dull in the extreme
This faculty—while but a partial gleam
Of bright originality he shows—
And no poetic tendency e'er glows
Within his brain's dark chambers; or no turn
For painting, sculpture, there in raptures burn!
With quite as good an ear for music, still
In composing he evinces little skill;
And many other points of difference
As great, exist between the two; 't is thence
The line of demarcation is made clear.)
The intermediate types distinct appear
In color, feature, form, and attributes
Progressive, even as they 're shown in brutes—
From low to high, and higher still, they 're seen
In man. We also see, there was, between
The production of each varied species,
In the earth's temperature a sure decrease,
Evolving new conditions, so, to bring
The next advancing type within the ring.

And thus, the next above the Negro, is
The Malay. Of a blackish brown is his
Complexion, broad his nose, and coarse and straight
His hair. Inhabitant of all the great
Broad chain of islands in the Southern Sea,
And most of the East Indian isles is he.
And scarcely less a savage than the first
Of *homo*, in his roving life and thirst
For wild adventure. And his skull is found
By the phrenologist, but to abound
In characters, which tho' they plainly tell
Of energy and courage, yet as well
Of stubbornness and harshness there that be,
And intellectual incapacity
Extreme, combined with selfishness :
While every talent requisite to bless
And to improve mankind, defective is ;
And ideality is so small in his
Development, that 't is not strange we find
Him in the social scale so far behind
His European brethren. And it is
Because the animal preponderates, that his
Cannibalistic habits operate ;
For most of these savage hordes will satiate

7

Their appetite for blood, and roast and eat,
Not only enemies, but—to complete,
If possible, their barbarism—make
Their bestial meals on infants ; or they take
Revenge in this way, on absconding slaves,
Nor lay restrictions on the act by halves.
And like atrocities prove them to be
Not far removed above the brute.

                        We see
The next advance in human order, lies
Within that land arched o'er by Western skies,
Where giant mountain ranges fortified
The wide-spread plains, and the exultant tide
Of grand Niagara shouted forth its praise
To the Most High ! and gave, in rainbow rays,
An everlasting arch, as covenant
Of Peace to be o'er that broad land extant,
When the vast wilderness should, as the rose,
Bloom in serene, majestical repose ;
The tomahawk and scalping-knife give way
Before the march of empire—the noonday
Sun of civilization !

                Yes, 'tis He,
The Red Man of the forest, now, that we

Must introduce upon the theater
Of mortal life. For he was, we infer
From doubtless proofs that nature gives, the third
Species of mankind—and surely born to herd
Where range the bear, and elk, and buffalo.
Remove him from his forest home, in wo
Untold you steep him ; for the glorious light
Of the great Sun, the sparkling stars of night,
The springing sapling and the russet brown
Of autumn's leaf, the meadow's emerald down,
The flight of swallows in the early spring,
The changing plumage of each warbler's wing;
Each varied garb that Nature dons at will,
Each mighty river and each tiny rill ;
Each footprint on the forest's path of leaves,
Or curious house of silk the insect weaves;
Each line of fog above a water-course,
Or blasted pine, or foaming torrent, hoarse
With screaming to the rocks; each blade of grass
That waves a welcome when the wild winds pass,
And every tree, shrub, bush, or bended twig,
Is to his eye with nature's teachings big !
The only volume on whose page he 'll look
Is *her* illimitable, mighty book;

The only logic that his reason heeds,
Is to divine all motives by their deeds;
His only creed (not versed in written word),
To "look thro' nature up to nature's God!"
    In this untutored forest child, we see
High reverence for an unknown Deity—
A great pervading Spirit! by whose power
And will, all things live out their destined hour.
A mighty Spirit! who not only gives
The earthly lodge wherein each warrior lives,
The grand old woods where he may track the deer,
The prairie's herds for his amusement here—
But, in that land beyond the setting sun,
Where each Brave goes when mortal combat's
      done,
He spreads the "Happy Hunting-Grounds" for
      his
Red children! O, let us despise not this
High prompting in the savage heart, which tells
Of life beyond the grave! What tho' there swells
From his bloodthirsty lip, the wild war-whoop,
And in fierce torture he disdains to stoop
To supplication—tho' he's treacherous,
Revengeful, cruel, cunning; still, with us,

Who claim to be enlightened, he must share
A meed of praise; for rude and wild as are
His habits, still he reverences all things
Which appertain to Deity, and brings
The human standard nearer to the goal
Where the immortal promptings of the soul
Are heard thro' the dull clay.

                True, that with him,
We find this principle is sadly dim
In moral aptitudes; and but arrays
The life to come with hue of mortal days,
And crowned with pleasures for the pulse of sense
To throb to—not the heavenly raptures, whence
The soul of intellect drinks in new light!
But shaded with the drapery of earth's night,
When the long-dormant spirit first begins
To plume itself for higher flight, and wins,
In the mere effort, glimpses of a sphere
Of happier being than surrounds it here—
Of immortality and endless bliss,
In higher realms when toil is o'er in this!
And if that future is thus clothed with joys,
That here below please with their gilded toys;
'Tis that the spirit yet is in its youth,

Nor reached the portal of its manhood's truth;
But trammeled with dull matter's leading-strings,
Which blend their earthly hues with heavenly
    things,
Thus coloring all its high imaginings—
It looks to that bright land to come, as one
Of animal enjoyment. Yet, begun,
The soul's high questioning in the Indian's breast,
Which bids it ask a higher, better rest
Than earth affords, and seek a God above
The wooden deity of Pagan love;
An All-wise God that made all things; not one,
By *man* constructed from a block or stone.
    And surely here are dawnings of a light
That yet should chase the blackness of the night
Of Heathenism, and progressing on
To broader daylight, fall in rays upon
The sacred mount whereon the living God
Gave to enlightened man his holy Word!
When Sinai's Hill in bright effulgence shone,
And to the ripened creature of his own
Progressive work, he gave his laws supreme,
To govern ALL, when full and wide the stream
Of golden glory, from the coming Sun

Of Christianity, should fall upon
The desert's palm, the islands of the sea,
The bright, " all-perfect day " that's yet to be,
When kindreds, nations, tongues, with rapt accords,
Shall own him "King of kings and Lord of
    lords!"
   The next advancing human grade, to these,
America's wild aborigines,
Is the Mongolian type, and perfect found,
Within the guarded, walled, forbidden ground
Of the Celestial Empire; where the eye
Of curiosity in vain may pry
To gain the secret of each quaint device,
Or queer contrivance; where chop-sticks and rice,
Souchong and pig-tails flourish; and the Sun,
High on his amber throne, is looked upon
As the Omnipotent, Omniscient One!
The idol of their worship.
                Nor can we,
To whom more light's been given, fail to see
In this idolatry, a beauty still;
For what more calculated is, to fill
The mind with awe, sublimity, than yon
Bright orb, whose fiery feet glide noiseless on

The sapphire walls of space? whose glowing
    eyes
Bring morn's soft blushes to the pale-faced skies;
Whose golden locks fall in a yellow rain
To fructify and fertilize each plain;
Whose breathings warm unseal the flowers' closed
    lips,
And opening leaf, unfolding blossom, sips
The mild, ethereal nectar, till it blooms
In glowing raiment—all, from night's dark
    tombs
Rising to matins pure, devotional—
Each morning's praises, resurrectional,
That float from lawn and grove, mount, vale and
    plain,
When Death's twin-sister, Sleep, gives up again
Her charge, and Sol's bright wand sweeps back
    the pall
Of darkness from the earth's green couch, and all
Of animated nature in the grand
Anthem join, to hail his advent bland,
As up the orient's jeweled steps he hies,
Day's light-crowned king, whose throne is in the
    skies!

No wonder, then, that man, by reason taught
To look for cause where'er effect is wrought,
Should, in his primitive intelligence,
Turn to that orb's refulgent splendor, whence
All things are touched with glory, and there
　　find
Presumptive evidence of power, combined
With light, life-giving attributes and heat
Dispensing properties—in fact, complete
Investments of each wondrous quality,
Unscientific minds to Deity
Ascribe—and learn to love and worship, this
The source of every blessing known in his
Experience.
　　　　　　This worship still will last
Until the heavy cloud the night has cast—
The night of mental darkness—parts its fold,
As glimmers from the better time, foretold
In prophet vision, rend the mist to let
The daylight in, whose rising Sun will set
Not; but widening to a broad stream
Of living glory, brightening in the gleam
Of light divine, shall flow o'er every land,
And "Bramah" fall at the Divine command!

Unhallowed Ganges' waves give up the ghost
Of buried Paganism; and the host
Of heathen, at Messiah's feet lay down
Their impious rites, and own the Thorny Crown
As brighter gem than "Vishnu's" diamond eyes;
And feel within their souls, more merit lies
In crucifying selfish passions, than
In fanatic prostrations in the van
Of Juggernaut's triumphal car!

       Roll on,
O Earth! and haste the time—for see, upon
The mount the watchman stands, and waits to hail
The coming light, whose noonday shall prevail,
When ALL shall join the anthem : "Blessed is he
That cometh in the name of the Lord!" and be
Bound with the cords of love and unity!

 We now come to the last, best type of all
The human race, upon this rolling ball,
Spontaneously formed: the Caucasian.
In color, form, proportions, we may scan
All other species, none with this compare;
For elegance symmetrical we there
With beauty find combined; at least, what WE
Consider such; for other people see

With other eyes—as the stained fingers, lips
Of indigo, black brows and red toe-tips
Of the Arabian belle; the crippled feet
Of Chinese beauty; and the most complete
Of checker-boards the Hottentot imprints
Upon her body, in decided tints
Of red and black, to captivate the eye;
The Greenland women's blue and yellow dye
With which they stain their faces; and
The tattooed beauties on the golden strand
Of the Pacific Ocean, plainly tell;
And also, of barbaric tastes that dwell
In human bosoms. For in these we find
No homage paid to mighty, godlike mind!
'Tis in the true Caucasian type we see
Alone, this principle complete, to be
The means, as time progresses, to subdue
The savage, quell the rude, and plant the true
And perfect principles of mortal life;
And barbarism, butchery, and strife,
Will be remembered only as the clouds
Which vail the sunrise, when earth's mist en-
    shrouds
The couch of morn with waving draperies gray;

But, as the warm, bright sun (like truth) away
To the high zenith springs, his piercing ray
Parts the dun curtain, and lets in the light,
And to the dark dominions of the night,
The cloud-like mist descends; so mind will yet
O'er matter triumph; and the world forget
In the bright future that is still to be,
That superstition, wrong, and cruelty
E'er marred the human race!
                              But all in time
This happy change will be. The passing chime
Of centuries must sound the dirge of each
Old fallacy or rotten creed, to teach
Immortal truths to man! Bigots may *preach*
Of universal charity and love,
The while their *lives* the contrary doth prove—
Or rear His standard as the Prince of Peace!
And claim to be disciples, yet ne'er cease
To throw the gauntlet at their fellow-man
Who different views has of Almighty plan;
Or place a stumbling-block where humble feet
Would climb, to bend before the mercy-seat;
And clothe their king with thunders such as Jove
Would hurl—not sweet, forgiving smiles of love,

To lure the sinner back to beaten track—
But with the torturing whip, the scourge, the rack
Of fierce anathema, pour forth a blast
Of dark revenge to be, for errors past,
Taken by Him, the *God of Mercy!*

                      See,
When the bleeding Savior hung upon the tree,
Upon his foes he cast his pitying eyes,
Then raised them meekly to the lowering skies,
And prayed: " Father, forgive them, for they know
Not what they do!" And this the love below—
This the bright spirit which o'er earth must sweep
Her radiant wings, her tireless vigils keep,
Ere lambs with lions couch—ere man for man
Feels as for self! Meek charity the van
Must take in human hearts, and tender, pitying love,
For weak mortality—ere, like a dove,
Sweet Peace, with all her blessings in her train,
Will soft descend, and, like the summer's rain,
Waken to life the flowers of gentleness,
Dear buds of hope to comfort and to bless,
While seeds of promise quicken fast to life
Beneath her genial influence—which strife,
With harsh breathings, else had chilled.

O man!
Thy brother's *nature* strictly, strictly scan,
Ere censuring him; and then, pause, still pause,
And for his weakness, mayhap, a cause
Will show itself, which will your pity wake,
And banish hatred for compassion's sake
Thus, in your heart you'll plant a goodly seed,
To bring forth tenfold for the spirit's need;
To bear immortal fruit whose bright'ning bloom
Will gild thy passage to the darksome tomb,
And branching there, to brighter skies, will spread
In fadeless laurels o'er your victor head!
For, who so great a conqueror, as he
O'er *self* victorious? and who yet can see
A *fellow-being* in the outcast one
Whom the self-righteous Pharisee doth shun,
And by a word of kindness, aptly said,
Pour balm on wounds that long have inly bled;
Heal the dark sore of sin by gentle word,
And lead an erring brother back to God!
    These, the conditions, which to man will bring
The ethereal mildness of Millennium spring,
When human hearts with gentle pity flow,
And brother seeks to heal a brother's wo,

And o'er a brother's weakness drop a tear
Instead of meeting it with scoff and jeer—
For *all* are mortal, and all flesh is prone
To wander ; but, when mighty mind shall own
Dominion, and shall join with love and faith
To conquer sin, then, then the victor's wreath
Shall crown mortality ; and man below
Foretaste the joys celestial, which glow
Where disembodied souls, from matter free,
Expand and brighten thro' eternity !
Where the glad spirit, on its new-born wings
Escaped the binding cord of earthly things,
Looks back on sin's dark night as sorrow past,
And hails the welcome light that's dawned at
    last,
When naught can stay its upward flight.
                  The soul—
No more, by weight of animal control,
Compelled to sit in judgment on the deeds
Of the poor, erring body—far exceeds
In splendor, what the eye or heart of man
Has ever dreamed of—in its reaching span
To grasp the good, the beautiful, the pure ;
And when 't is landed on the crystal shore

Of the Eternal River, freed from sense
And all its penalties—expansive, thence,
It brighter glows with gems of thought refined,
And stands, th' embodiment of glorious mind;
That link, which God designed should unite man
With angels, in his grand, progressive plan!
   And God's great laws, unceasing, slow, and
     sure,
Are working earth's redemption evermore;
Tho' man, in his blind ignorance, fails to see
In many things, the hand of Deity
That's molding up the plastic clay of thought
To higher points of interest, and fraught
With rich revealings—Truth's unfolding light
Intensifying, as its radiance bright
Rolls back the darkness of the mental night
Shrouding the past. Old things give way to new,
As the world waxeth to the full and true
Perception of the grand and beautiful,
The reasonable and the dutiful;
And manners, customs, habits, feelings change,
As greater scope is given the mind to range
In nature's storehouses, there to explore
Her mysteries and read her ancient lore,

And see in all things wisdom, love, and power,
Assigning to each blade of grass, each flower,
Or stately tree, each rain-drop, spring, or flood,
Its portion toward the universal good ;
And every insect, animal, or race,
Its fitting attributes and proper place,
To exist *while needed*, then, to pass away ;
And new conditions, with the old's decay,
Dawn into being.
     View our own loved land,
By nature fashioned in appointments grand.
Once, its bold rocks, huge forests, mighty lakes,
High towering mountains, and deep tangled
  brakes,
Wide-spreading prairies, flowing rivers, free,
All a vast wilderness was known to be,
Where the fierce wolf couched in his rocky lair
And roamed the panther, and wild grizzly bear ;
Or Red Man tracked the elk with bended bow,
While timid deer lurked in the covert low ;
And flashing from Niagara's sheet of light
The " council fire," reflected clear and bright ;
Or where the Mississippi valley spread
In wild luxuriance, the measured tread

8

Of painted warriors broke the deep repose,
As the exultant "death-song" fierce, uprose
From some poor victim at the fiery stake,
Who scorned one faint entreaty there to make;
And where the mighty river wanders o'er
His clayey bed—each bluff or wood-crowned shore
Echoed the shrill war-whoop, both fierce and
    free;
Yet, thro' the thick foliage of each tree,
The peaceful calumet sent wreathy smoke,
And songs of savage joy the silence broke.
But now, the Red Man's reign is o'er—his day
Has run its limit—and away, away
From earth he's swept, no longer needed there;
But, with the wolf, the panther, and the bear,
He flies before that onward march, which sows
The wilderness with myrtle and the rose.
He leaves that lovely land, designed to be
The cradling-place of heaven-born Liberty !
Where for a time he flourished; but where now
The leveling ax, the saw, the spade, the plow,
Have spread broad fields, and towns and cities
    rise,
With gilded spires that point to brighter skies !

This noble Western World, fair Freedom's car!
Had higher destiny, more glorious far,
Than the rude savages' broad hunting-ground
To be, thro' circling ages' ceaseless round.
But still, when haunt of creatures fierce and wild,
No fitter habitant than "forest child"
(Which cognomen's the Indian's birthright, clear),
Could be by Wisdom placed as ruler here.
No longer wanted—see, he passes on
His sunset path, where myriad Braves have gone;
And, let us hope, to find that spirit-rest
In the Hereafter's regions of the blest!
    Here, then, is seen how manifold the ways
Of Providence! We, in enlightened days,
Who o'er the past send a far-reaching glance,
Can see each step progressively advance
To the *still distant but still nearing* goal
Where sense will yield supremacy to soul;
Where present wrong will turn to future right,
And day succeed the gloomy, darksome night;
Can see Truth's glimmer, faint and far, 't is true—
But o'er the dead Old World 't will burst with new
And higher glory, when our rising star
Shall culminate, and spread its light afar;

And ancient empires, thrones, and kingdoms quake,
As shouts of "freedom" from this broad land
    break—
Atlantic's shores echo the watchword wide,
And broad Pacific's ever-flowing tide
Bears the hosanna on to distant lands,
And mighty floods, all-joyful, clap their hands,
And spread glad tidings far from Pole to Pole,
Where wild winds blow or foaming oceans roll,
Lighting a spark, a quenchless spark, to rise,
When once 't is kindled, flaming to the skies!
A tiny ball, which, gaining as it goes,
Falls in an avalanche like mountain snows,
And with resistless force sweeps all aside,
And buries wrong, oppression, pomp, and pride,
Beneath its pure, unsullied, spotless garb,
Heaven's matchless ermine, man's protective barb,
The banner of the just, the good, the true,
Which yields to mind and soul their being's due!
   "From little acorns mighty oaks arise!"
This proverb fleeting time still verifies.
The seedling of a giant tree was sown,
When the stanch Pilgrims freely left their own
Fair land to tread these Western wilds, and raise

Unchecked their prayers and unrebuked their
  praise!
Self-exiled from their homes, with hearts as true
As finest-tempered steel, to brave (tho' few
Their numbers) all the savage hosts, before
They'd yield their right their Maker to adore
As conscience dictated. The germ, thus laid
In genial soil, now spreads a grateful shade
From wide-spread foliage, o'er the happy land
Where Freedom's banner floats on breezes bland;
Where a blest nation rears its honored head
From conquered Despotism's ashes red;
The eagle, Liberty, on heavenward wings,
Soars on triumphant, or exultant sings,
From cloud-capped eyrie, anthems grand that
  swell
To pæans glorious, and sound the knell
Of dark Oppression—till each fettered soil
Looks up from gyves and serfdom's forced toil,
To catch the refrain rolling o'er the sea,
And brave hearts echo, "FREE! WE WILL BE
  FREE!"
  Yes! Yes! ALL will be free in time—in time;
But Liberty's a plant that every clime

Must raise *spontaneously*, ere a firm hold
Its root can take! All *forcing*, we are told,
Produces sickly growth; and Nature, true
To all her instincts, thus, must first induc
The mind with proper attributes, and give
The energies for freedom's plant to live
And flourish; then the pruning-knife may be
Applied, to lop from the yet budding tree
Its useless branches, to condense its strength,
And goodly foliage 'twill yield at length;
Nourished by proper soil, its growth will be
Proportionate to any native tree,
That under genial airs and kindred skies,
Lifts its crowned head with plumes of varied dyes,
And to the passing breeze may bend, not break—
The forest's king, which tempests fail to shake!
With heart of oak and brow undimmed by age
'Twill stand, the youthful hero and the sage;
Firm at the core, but pleasing to the eye—
The green-bay-tree, heaven-grafted, Liberty!
    The mind has its conditions: soul and sense
Must work harmonious, ere progressive thence
Springs ripe fruition. Not where thistles thrive
Will plenteous crops be gathered! Man, alive

Tho' he may be to his high attributes,
Which place him far, so far above dumb brutes,
Must feel the promptings of immortal mind
And will indomitable; these, combined,
The despot's gilded throne can overthrow;
For mind is power and will is might, below!
And when this dual force is brought to bear,
The strongest fetters burst—dissolve in air;
Earth's adamantine monarchies give way,
And Freedom's sun pours down its golden ray,
As broad it shines on our own land to-day!

Blest land! the honored birthplace and the grave
Of him who would have given his life to save
Thy sons from despotism's iron rule,
But scorned to be a tyrant's slave or tool.
O, shout exultant to thy peaceful skies
His name! and as the sound still echoing flies
From fame's high mount, 't will give—that patriot
     cry—
A mold for gods to fashion heroes by!
For where's the land can boast another son,
To equal thine, thy noble Washington?
O, proudly rear thy head, "Queen of the West,"
And own thyself, o'er all, supremely blest;

And keep the trust his lips to thee have given
As thou wouldst answer it before High Heaven.
For see, a cloud, no bigger than man's hand,
Is creeping o'er thy atmosphere so bland,
To spread and blacken the fair soil afar
With all the horrors of intestine war,
And civil feud; where brother brother meets
As mortal foe, and enmity completes
What anarchy began.   Pause, brethren, pause!
Respect each other's rights, our country's laws,
Ere wickedly attempting to undo
The floodgates of rank discord, and imbrue
With native blood our rising empire's sod—
Once spake that country's savior next to God!

  And what this threatened wo, this tiny cloud
Whose spreading will our prospects _ fair en-
      shroud?
The spirit of Dictation! that would wrest
Another's right of thought from his own breast,
And sever cords of unity and love
Whose links were twined in the bright realms
      above;
Whose rights were purchased by our fathers brave
Who nobly fought and bled their land to save,

And dying, left the heritage to those
As brothers joined, but now, almost as foes
Arrayed with hostile feelings, just because
They differ in regard to freedom's laws;
And hot, vituperative, random speech
Is rolling ever to increase the breach,
Till discord riots o'er the tottering land.
And, as a house divided can not stand—
So, with these discords, the broad Union shakes;
The arching firmament with terror quakes,
Lest from our banner's spangled azure fold
Its sister stars should leave their glorious hold,
And 'mid the ruin of their universe
Die out in darkness! Heaven forbid, this curse
Should ever blot our fair escutcheon!

       List!

Ye sowers of dissension, nor insist
That you've the right to point your brethren's
  course,
Which, should they follow, still would lead to worse
Conditions than exist—list to the voice
Of reason! and not rashly make the choice
That severs all our bonds of brotherhood;
Clipped by rank Faction's discontented brood

9

Of meddlers, cloaked in piety's broad garb,
To hide the point of foul dissension's barb,
And under pretense of philanthropy
Plant hatred, violence, and anarchy
In kindred soil.   Ah! 't is no feeling pure,
(An empty boast), but simply to insure
A right to dictate to the rest, and show
The North will teach the South the way to go!
'T is not true horror of "*vile slavery*"
Calls forth this bombast of great bravery,
Or sympathy for the poor Negro lends
A strength to wield the battle-ax, and tends
To lessen the deep horror of these broils,
These family dissensions and turmoils!
O brothers, ALL, both North and South, I pray
Give ear to me, and hearken to my lay,
The while I prove to thee, the hand of God
Holds over Africa the divining rod,
To lift from barbarism's horrid hold
Her sunk humanity, whose hidden gold
Were worthless else, with savage dross o 'ergrown,
Which to subdue, no better means are known
Than those of a judicious slavery.
Not the foul bondage coined by knavery

And represented to exist where rolls
The white-capped waves of bursting cotton bolls,
And fields of sugar-cane, luxuriant spread
Beneath a fiery sun's fierce, burning tread;
But such a thralldom as superior powers
May lay on weaker, in this world of ours,
When soul and sense unite to point the way
To better things, to *humanize* the clay
Of savagism! And this, *God permits*
To be, while needed, as a means that fits
The Negro to receive his Word, and kiss
The chastening rod that points to future bliss !

  We must deny the Bible's holy word
To say that slavery came not from God!
On its blest pages read we duty there
To *slave and master* both assigned. And where
The palmy days of Israel rose, 't is shown
That slavery existed; and 't is known
The Christian Dispensation recognized
Its justice, *now* so basely scandalized.
And tho' the dawnings of a brighter day
May glimmer from the distant future, say,
Is the Negro *yet* endowed aright
To govern self? And what (we ask in quite

A humble spirit), what is to become
Of him, if from his comfortable home
Emancipated, he is forced to flee?
Left to himself, a savage he will be!
This has been tried—in St. Domingo now
View his barbarity; or else, he 'll bow
To some superior savage race, and be
By greater force destroyed.

                    Ah! happier, he
Well fed, well clothed, well cared for in that land
Which fanatic reformers deeply brand
(Those transcendental bigots, who can't see
The never-failing ways of Deity,
Nor hear the voice that in the wilderness
Calls night and day the means of all redress,
And in the *groaned-o'er*, falsely-pictured fate
Of Africa, makes clear the path, and straight,
For Him to enter—the Almighty One!)
They 've yet to learn, the work that is begun
By Providence, is never left undone;
For God's will works in a mysterious way,
Which men unconscious to themselves, obey,
And coming light will part all dark'ning screens,
And prove the end to justify the means;

And when the proper time has come, we'll see
(What is not now the case) the Black will be
Fitted, as is the White man, to be free!

We'll take a backward glance, and try to trace
The rise of Slavery in the human race,
At least, as far as mortal records show—
And see what horror, agony, and wo,
At one time stamped it with an iron heel;
Then, view it *now*, and every heart will feel
The present age is surely leading on
To strike the hidden path, where lies the stone
So vainly sought by alchemists of old,
To turn all baser metals to pure gold—
Designed the crowning glory yet to be
Of man, the godlike scepter with which he
Will right all wrongs, all grievances redress,
Succor all weakness, soothe all dire distress,
And plant the banner of the just and true
To guard a world! to conquer and subdue
All barbarisms, despotisms, bold;
And turn these base alloys to finest gold!
Gold in the furnace tried — like that which
    gleams
From Free America in radiant beams,

To light the Old World's feeble steps along
The path her brave young son has nobly gone,
And in the footsteps of yon orb of fire
From East to West, has mounted higher, higher
Till in the zenith a broad noonday flame
Lights all the glorious road by which he came,
And writes in golden characters his fame!

Slavery.

THE Book of books we confidently quote
In reference to the past, doth plainly note
The fact, that slavery existed when
Good Noah (he who found above all men,
Grace in the eyes of God) dwelt in the land
Deluged, 'tis said, by the Divine command;
For in the malediction breathed upon
His younger and his most irreverent son,
These words he used: " Accursed shall Canaan be,
A servant's servant ever shall be he
Unto his brethren,"—and by this, 'tis shown,
That servitude 'mong men is fairly known
To have existed ere the floods of heaven
Poured forth, we're told, upon an unforgiven,
Corrupt, and wicked generation; for,
'Twas shortly after that fierce watery war
Was said to have been waged, that Ham provoked
His parent's ire, who vengeance dire invoked

(103)

On him and all his progeny—and hence
We've grounds for the belief, that Slavery thence
Has progressed 'mong the nations of the earth,
And claims this far-removed and ancient birth.

   Nimrod's the first that dealt in slaves, that we
Can trace such dealings to. We're told, that he
Became a mighty one upon the earth—
"A mighty hunter before the Lord!" Now,
    worth
Is given by commentators, to this clause,
Proportionate to all translations' flaws—
They give the literal meaning thus: " Of *men*
A mighty hunter he became ;" for then,
By Scripture it appears, his conquests were
Immense, the territories of Ashur
Invaded were by him—he seized upon
That far-famed city, Ancient Babylon,
And made it what it was, the capital
Of the first kingdom in the world! And shall
We err in saying, that the captives ta'en
In war by him, were forced to remain
Bond-servants to the conqueror !

               And 't is seen
'Twas so—for seventy years scarce rolled between

The death of Nimrod and good Abraham's birth,
Yet in that Patriarch's age there was no dearth
Of servitude—in his own house were born
Three hundred and eighteen slaves; and on that
    morn
When Siddam's vale rang with the din of war,
And battle's issues, on the " Four Kings' " car
Of triumph, captive placed his brother's son—
He armed his " trained servants," every one,
Pursued the conquerors unto Dan—by night
Smote them, and still pursued to Hobah quite,
Nor ceased till he'd recaptured all the spoil
(He and his servants) of the bloody toil,
And brought back women, goods, and *people*,
    too,
To Sodom's king—who generously, in view
To reward him, said : " The *persons* give to me,
And take the goods to thyself." By this, we see
That each one thought the conqueror had a right
To hold as slaves all captives ta' en in fight.
And many other scriptural texts will show
How valued then all bondsmen were ; for so,
The sacred writer Abraham's wealth describes—
He says, that he had of men-servants, tribes,

And sheep and oxen, and he-asses, and
Maid-servants, and she-asses, to command;
And camels.   Such was also Jacob's dower,
And Isaac's estimated wealth and power.

    That Slavery was authorized by law
Among the Israelites, we find no flaw
In Holy Writ to contradict; we see
There, also, how all servants were to be
Treated.   First: They were to be bought alone
Of heathen—for, if a poor Jew was known
To sell himself either for food, or debt,
The limits of his servitude were set
To expire upon the year of Jubilee,
If after six years' bondage he would be
Considered still a servant—then, to show
That from this service he declined to go,
The master, with an awl, bored fast his ear
To the door-post, to show that he would here
Remain a slave till jubilee's blest year.
But slaves for life, those bought and sold again,
Or which as fixed inheritance remain
In families forever, were of those
Taken in war, the heathen, strangers, foes.
Says Moses : " Both thy bondmen and bondmaids

Shall be of the heathen." And he further
    adds :
" And ye shall take them as inheritance
For your children after you." And if (as
    chance
Might be), a master beat a slave to death,
He was not doomed by the unswerving breath
Of justice stern, to pay the penalty
Such crime exacts from high and low degree
In human courts to-day—but simply was
Punished proportionate unto the cause,
As this was deemed sufficient. Such was then
The power that man held o'er his fellows, men.

    Ah! happy we to have outlived the time,
And reached the borders of a milder clime,
Where mercy and compassion's wreaths entwine,
And justice and humanity combine
To lighten fetters forged by direst need,
Pour balm on wounds destined so long to bleed,
Till bondage by sweet sympathy made light,
Sees not its shackles, unless thrust in sight
By self-styled friends! who rattle loud the
    chains,
And the poor victim writhes 'neath fancied pains;

The while these wolves clothed in their sheepskin
    garbs,
Sink deep their fangs, their sharp and poisoned
    barbs,
Which with their victim's life-blood mingles, and
The tares of discontent on every hand
Spring up, and choke the better fruit whose bloom
Was lighting the dark passage to the tomb,
Till these rank weeds o'erspread the kindly soil
And crushed the produce of a better toil ;
Planting a bitter enmity 'twixt those—
Master and slave—who never should he foes ;
Tightening the latter's bonds and locking up
The former's sympathies.   And this, the cup
Of bitterness, these meddlers mix for those
Poor idiots, who know not friends from foes !

    Ah well ! there is a proverb old, doth say
That mighty " Rome was not built in a day."
And let us hope these bigots yet will see
How false the path they've chosen.   If to free
The Negro is their *only* end and aim—
And such the generous purpose they would claim—
We 'll trust to time's all-powerful, potent test,
To prove their error, leaving God the rest !

His laws unceasing will work out their end,
However men may strive or fools contend;
And when they cry, " A lion's at the door,"
Before we fly we 'll wait to hear him roar,
Nor conjure beast-with *longer ears* to be
The king at whose loud voice all creatures flee;
And go unflinching on our path, with faith
That sober second thought will lay the wraith
Of troubled Abolitionism low—
That wandering spirit with perturbed brow!

    Now turn we to that land by classic song
And Homer's verse, immortal made among
The lands of earth ! We find, that Slavery there,
Despite its orators and heroes fair,
Existed, and atrocities most foul
Were perpetrated; while the victim's howl
Of anguish, music was most sweet to hear,
To the ferocious conqueror's bestial car.
Such were the habits of the Greeks of old.
And even in Alexander's time, we're told,
That when he had rased Thebes, he seized and
    sold
Men, women, children, all for slaves. But still,
The Spartans were most cruel—for with skill

They trained the Lacedemonian youth
To practice all achievements void of truth,
Purposely to deceive and butcher those
Poor captives seized as slaves from out their foes.
And this was but to show their progress in
The stratagems of massacre, and win
A base applause for deeds of wantonness
'Gainst those who had no means of just redress.

    Even Rome, imperial city of the East!
Could boast but little over these—at least
Till Christianity's mild rays shed holier light
To turn brute force and question wrong and right.
For the blood-stained arena's gory flow,
The dark, inhuman, gladiatorial show;
The stiffened corpse dragged thro' the circus' round
(First scourged to death the slave was, and then
     bound
In his hand a fork in gibbet form)'; the dread
And brutal Vedius Pollio's conduct; still must shed
A nameless horror o'er those barbarous times,
And cause us bless the ring of happier chimes.

    In Sicily, during the commonwealth,
Masters, to keep their slaves from march of
     stealth,

Branded their foreheads with an iron hot;
And one slaveholder (Damophilus), not
Content with this security, shut fast
His slaves at night in prisons close, then pass'd
Them out like beasts to daily work at morn.
Thank Heaven, we now can hail a brighter dawn,
Tho' fleecy clouds *may* hang upon its brow,
Their silver edges tell how bright the glow
Behind them—a radiance which shall pierce
The farthest limits of the universe,
When rolling time shall reach the point at last
Where misty doubts, into Faith's ocean cast,
Resolve themselves to pearls of truth and love,
To gleam and scintillate in courts above!

A milder form of Slavery prevailed
Among the ancient Germans. This assailed
Not wantonly its subjects, nor imposed
Undue exactions; slaves were not exposed
To cruel treatment. Attached to the soil,
And working and improving it their toil,
With tending cattle, they could neither be
Made articles of commerce nor yet free.
The only ones that could be bought and sold,
Were freemen who had lost themselves for gold;

For it was no uncommon thing to see
An ardent gamester stake his liberty
Upon a dice's turn ; the victor then
Could sell his property to other men.
But the condition of the slave still seems
To have been much better than the savage gleams
Thrown from the annals of the polished Greeks
And Romans.

    Then, by one of those strange freaks
Of retrogression, which sometimes exist
'Mong nations on this "island in the mist;"
The Anglo-Saxons seem not to have been
So honorable in this traffic as we've seen
Were their Teutonic forefathers. As when
Alfred (he, surnamed "the Great") pass'd 'mong
  men
A law forbidding purchase of a *man*,
A *horse*, an *ox*, without a voucher: can
We doubt, the statute was but to prevent
The *stealing* of such property ? This bent
Must have prevailed to have called forth the law.
And, to apply an almost worn-out "saw:"
"'T is a poor rule that will not work both ways,"
Men must have been property in those days,

Otherwise, why steal them?

A species too
Of slavery, alike to that which thro'
The German States held sway, existed in
The Kingdom of Great Britain, till within
The last three centuries. And this is seen
From a commission issued by the Queen,
The famous Queen Elizabeth of yore,
In fifteen hundred and seventy-four,
Inquiring 'bout the lands and goods of all
Her *bondmen* and *bondwomen* in Cornwall,
Devon, Somerset, and Gloucester,
In order that they might compound with her
For manumission, and enjoy their lands
And goods as freemen. So, the matter stands
Till now. A work of later years has been
To free the Colliers, Salters—who were seen
To have endured a wretched serfdom, worse
Than negro-slavery's much quoted curse.
Doomed in dark mines, to wear life's threads
    away,
Robbed of God's precious gift, the light of day!
And even their wretched children born to share
The curse, which shut them from sunshine and air,

10

Till little better than the grub, they crept
Thro' their dark holes in mother earth, or slept
A sort of waking sleep—for intellect,
Crushed by the nightmare, darkness, can't reflect
The hues prismatic which life-giving light
Calls forth victorious o'er the brooding night,
And in an apathetic torpor run
Their race, destined to end where it begun!
   So far, so good; and England acted well
In freeing those poor wretches doomed to dwell
In earth's dark bowels—for, of the same race
These sons of toil held with her equal place
In human grade—but stepped she not too far
In leaving her West India door ajar,
And vesting savages with powers and rights,
To equal sway with more enlightened Whites?
And what's the result, this vaunted labor free
Has brought to her?   Where once there used to
     be
Most ample stores of tropical produce,
The soil, from dire neglect and rank misuse,
Scarce yields supplies for home consumption—
     while
Fair Cuba's sugar-fields prolific smile;

Her green tobacco waves in fragrance sweet,
And fills the holds of many a noble fleet.
And why? Because *right* management and toil
Bring out the richness of the generous soil—
The White man's intellect, the Negro's strength,
Are brought to bear, and harvest comes at length.

But, as the Negro will not work unless
Compelled, why lay such monstrous, direful stress
Upon his slavery, which brings to him .
Comforts he'd never have the will to win
If left to himself? This, England knows full well,
And free Jamaica's sterile fields now tell,
The world would suffer for supplies of those
Commodities, on which it vainly throws
The obloquy of "slavery's products;" *while*
The want of them would hardly cause a smile,
If on "free labor" we'd depend, to give
These necessaries by which millions live.
For *White men* can not stand a tropic sun,
And *Blacks, by nature fitted for it*, won
Can never be by *hire* to do more work
Than will keep off starvation; they will *shirk*
(To use a Yankee phrase) all that they can,
Are naturally lazy to a man.

Why is it sinful, then, to take them from
The barbarous wilds of Afric, where they roam
But little else than brutes—and give them homes,
And turn to *men* these dark ungainly gnomes?
Will any other means ere civilize
These savages, beneath our Christian skies?
Or, setting that aside—must these fair lands
Remain as deserts 'neath our helpless hands,
When means are known on earth, if well employed,
To cause them yield what we've so long enjoyed?
Nor only us—the workers have their share;
Well fed, well clad, and taught both praise and
    prayer—
Saved from the darker horrors that await
Less fortunate companions in a state
Of barbarism still in their own land,
Stamped as it's always been with savage brand,
And made their being's aim to understand.
That Africa at any time was free
From the most horrid forms of slavery,
All history forbids us to suppose.
There, tribe 'gainst tribe, arrayed as mortal foes,
Enslave each other.   'Mong the ancient race
As far back as we've records left to trace,

Even to the era of the Trojan war,
We find Phœnicia trading with Lybia for
Her slaves ; and Carthage, which was known to be
No more than a Phœnician colony,
Following the customs of its parent state,
Still carried on the traffic with the great
Interior tribes of that wild, desert land,
Where burning sunbeams flow o'er parched sand,
And the tall palm-tree with its high plumed head,
Scarce deigns a strip of grateful shade to shed;
But miles of sterile, unproductive land
Stretch far and wide around on every hand,
With only here and there a little dot
Of verdure, a grass-grown and welcome spot
That marks a water-course; and which the cry
Of thirsty camel tells, ere man can spy,
That 't is the blest oasis which they near
To yield their worn-out strength its grateful cheer.

And still in modern times her sons are seen
Subjected unto bondage. They had been
Made slaves of by the nations of the earth
At a much earlier period than the birth
Of European slavery of the race.
'Tis proved beyond a doubt, that we can trace

A trade in slaves to have been carried on
By Arabs wild, previous to this, upon
The coast of Guinea—e'en some hundred years
Before the incursive Portuguese appears
Upon the western coast, or e'er had seen
A woolly-headed Negro. 'Twas between
The war of the Crusaders in the year
Eleven hundred (when it doth appear
That Europeans first obtained a sight
Of Africans, which caused their army quite
A burst of merriment), and that fierce time—
Some cycles back in rolling centuries' chime—
When Nubia's king, sore harassed by the host
Of bold Egyptian Arabs, who did boast
Mohammed as their God, agreed to send
By way of tribute—and also, to tend
Toward lessening these annoyances—a vast
Number of Nubian slaves to Egypt. Fast
To this covenant held, each year was he
Then forced to drain on neighboring bands; we
   see,
He bought the Blacks of Guinea, whom he
   paid
In tribute to the Calif—thus the trade

May have been said to have commenced abroad,
Tho' long prevailing 'mong each native horde
In the interior.
       That this was so,
To prove, we need no farther backward go
Than the last century. The Dahomans,
One of the wild interior's warlike clans,
Had never seen a White man till the year
Seventeen hundred and twenty-seven; and here,
Their prince and army met some travelers
In Sabi, and were so shocked, it appears,
At their complexion and their dress, they were
Afraid to approach them, and were heard demur
As to their being *men* until they spoke;
Then satisfied that it was not a joke,
They yet were much astonished when informed
That *these* were buyers of the slaves that swarmed
For purchasers upon the Guinea coast.
Yet these Dahomans, most inhuman, boast
Such horrid cruelties to such poor slaves
As chance they hold, that a wretch freely braves
The unknown good that may in foreign chains
Be found, to native bondage with its stains
Of cannibalism, its most monstrous rites,

Unholy usages and shocking sights !
Such is, we find, the present state of things
In Africa ; and this conviction brings
Us to the inquiry : Where will we see
In the world's annals, a community
Composed of Negroes, that have ever been
So well off as our slaves ?   Better ('t is seen
By the distress and want that wide prevailed
In late disastrous times, and fierce assailed
The working classes of the North) by far,
Is their condition, than nine-tenths that are
Compelled to earn their all by labor free ;
For, let a "panic" stop the wheels, and see,
The *poor* man is the sufferer ; no right
Has he to " daily bread," unless his mite
Of work is added to the general stock.
And, as "retrenchment" bids the master lock
His coffers, and reduce his working hands,
Minus employment, the poor laborer stands
But little chance of shutting his slight door
On wolf-like hunger's fierce and maddening
    roar.
Not so our well-fed Negroes. Housed and warm,
They, unconcerned, abide the wildest storm

That shakes the base of the commercial world,
Nor heed the rudest tempest ever hurled
From speculation's giddy hights.   For them
Decline of stocks no terror has; they stem
The tide of life, sure of a hand to save
From every 'whelming billow and each wave
Of want that o'er the working White man rolls.
Their bodily requirements met—their souls,
Exhumed from the foul rubbish and neglect
Of savage ignorance, can full reflect
The beams of Christianity's bright sun;
Showing how well the work that was begun
Long years ago for their advancement, is
Progressing to its end of future bliss!
   ' O Shame! where is thy blush,'' that in such
     cause
Wild fanatics should, 'spite their country's laws,
And in the face of verdict just, see flaws
To cavil at?   Such men would, doubtless, see
Motes in the eyes of Truth?   A class, a flea
Would choke, but who, without grimace or gag,
Can swallow camels whole!   For loud they brag
Of tireless efforts in behalf of those
Who 're well protected from privation's woes,

While brothers round them starve for want of
    work,
And sisters, under master fierce as Turk,
Stitch, for a pittance, their life-threads away,
Yet mourn they for the slave, more blest than
    they,
Who, free from care, with childlike confidence
Looks for protection, comfort (*competence*,
Compared to those poor creatures' ill supplies),
To him who seldom want or wish denies.
For the "good servant" knows his lord will yield
Increase to him whose talent in the field
Lies buried not—the laborer will find
He's worthy of his hire; and master kind
Supplies the mental force that can direct
The Negro's muscle.   Thus, our land is decked
With the rich crops by which we want defy,
And White and Black have plentiful supply.

    And yet this happy state of things must be
Made a vain pretext for rank anarchy,
Seditious speech, and wordy war, by those
Whose pretense *friendship* is, but who are foes
Of direst, deadliest import to our land
Blest in its own mild government to stand;

Which, with unholy zeal, they seek to change,
And all our articles of faith derange;
Assuming to themselves a paramount
Ability to dictate, o'er the Fount
Whence all our blessings are derived—and raise
A new law-code, a better form of praise
Than our forefathers gave, who left the soil
And Constitution without stain, when toil
For freedom ended. Wisely they assigned
Each one his place, nor thought, when they con-
　signed
The Negro to the ranks of servitude
(The fit condition for his nature rude),
The policy would ere be questioned. But
Our country's "faster" grown since then, and
　soot
O'er ivory soars in bigots' brains, who see
Not what a trial vaunted liberty
Becomes to Sambo, when he's forced to earn
By his own wits, his livelihood, and learn
To think for himself. [A phrase unknown
In his vocabulary.] They disown
All fair approaches to the truth, and seek
To cover purpose foul with aspect meek;

And if permitted, ne'er will cease, till all
This lovely land lies covered with a pall
Of darkness—and our glowing sun goes down
Behind a severed nation's gloomy frown!

    O! where the wisdom now to guide aright
The sinking ship of state, ere the dark night
That's hovering on the horizon's verge, sets in!
No second Washington, we fear, will win
A nation's grateful plaudits by a firm,
Consistent course of action; while the worm
That's sapping at our peace, works ceaseless on.
O! mighty Truth, arise! shed rays upon
Our glorious Constitution's outraged brow,
Nor let our native eagle's proud head bow,
His quivering wings fall listless by his sides,
That from Atlantic's to Pacific's tides
Spread their broad pinions—when, his eyry
    rent
From Alleghany's cloud-capped battlement
He looks abroad to seek another hight;
And on the one side stretches to his sight
New England's snow-crowned mounts and busy
    vales,
Her peopled cities and her homestead dales—

The cold, proud " North," hemmed in on every
    hand
By colleges and churches at command,
And all her hardy sons toiling untired
(As never *slaveling* toiled by *fear* inspired)
To heap bright ingots, or to strike a trade;
To drive a bargain, or mayhap a spade;
To dig an *idea* or potato patch—
No matter which, so gold they thereby hatch;
Or using powers which might be better spent,
In sowing broad-cast, seeds of discontent,
And loud declaiming 'gainst their sister, " South,"
Because she will not take from her own mouth.
The food on which she lives, and trust to Heaven
To shower down manna for her sins forgiven !
The while they see not what poor slaves they are
Themselves, chained in the van of Mammon's car,
To creeds and stereotyped ideas of right,
In spite of Truth's broad, plain, ungarnished light,
Which seeing, they won't see—a blindness worse
Than Nature's dark, unfathomable curse
Which lays a vail upon her beauteous face,
Thro' which no feature can her victim trace
But seeming nothingness and midnight's space—

And this too, while they claim to be but *just!*
Yet let the golden rule grow red with rust;
For, 't is not "as they would be done by," this
Invasion of another's premises—
Sees far away Ontario's waters blue,
Niagara's arch and sprays of silver dew,
Great Erie's waves breaking in ceaseless roar,
And fertile field, and wood, and rock-bound shore,
All fair to look upon.

                    Then turns him, where
The myrtle and magnolia scent the air,
And orange blossoms lend their sweets to roll
Above each bursting, downy cotton boll;
Where skies are blue and golden light pours down
In warm effulgence from Old Sol's bright crown,
And fires the blood of ancient chivalry
In heroes' veins, who boast a fair degree
Of that bright spirit which to woman gave
The homage of the good, the true, the brave!
And where SHE'S honored, there, as always
    seen,
The greatest moral excellence has been
And *that* she's honored in the sunny clime
Where citron ripens with the yellow lime,

Needs not be told—its noble sons full well
Attest her influence and own her spell,
Till each, thus purified, might lead the van
" To give the world assurance of a man !"—
Sees Mexico's broad gulf bearing upon
Its restless waves the tithes of commerce on,
And Mississippi's ever-flowing tides
Groaning 'neath products which its fertile sides
Yield in their vast luxuriance—sees far
And near, a happy people free from jar
Or discord, save the forced broils a band
Of sectionists spread thro' their peaceful land,
Willing to heed the *eleventh* commandment true,
" Mind your own business"—(not *your neighbor's*
    too,
As added and amended to this clause
By folks in higher latitudes, whose laws
Embrace a wider field)—with faith in man
And trust in God's supreme and hallowed plan
Which in the end will surely prove the right
As sure as day succeeds the darksome night!—
   Sees all this land, this broad and beauteous
    land,
Whose sons united, formed a goodly band;

But now the close-knit chain shows many chinks,
And hideous gaps are parting its firm links;
And clouds are vailing the horizon's blue,
And soon will darken all the sun's light too.
From North, from South, from East, from West,
        arise
These shadows o'er the brightly glowing skies,
Till all in vain he looks to find safe rest
Within the regions that his heart loves best;
Then, with a lowered crest and drooping eye,
He folds his wings and lays him down to die,
Rather than choose between the severing hosts
Whose name was "legion," and whose banner
        boasts
For motto: "One in many."   Ah! alas!
The golden bowl seems as 't were made of glass,
And waiting but the slightest blow to part
In minute fragments its full brittle heart!

    That slavery of the African will last
While Cotton's King, analogy must cast
The crowning vote to; for have we not seen
All things on earth subservient have been
To human needs, by wise, Almighty plan?
God's laws assisting the advance of man

Along the steep hill of progression.   See
How useful by this means the Black can be
Toward beautifying and adorning this
Fair earthly temple, to the praise of His
Omniscient name, the Architect supreme
Of the whole universe! who deigns a gleam
Of radiance to cast o'er savage man,
To rescue him from barbarism's ban,
And place him where his attributes will show
To best advantage, where his part below
He may act out, and thus assist the whole
Great human mass, whose bulk will ceaseless roll,
Till grain by grain it loses all its dross,
And rarefying with supernal gloss
'T will shine, the embodiment of truth and love,
And fitted for a higher march above
Dull matter—'t will, expanding, soar away,
To realms of glowing light and endless day!

   The reign of superstition is not o'er,
Altho' we boast more knowledge than of yore—
When bigots thus before the public eye
Can flaunt monstrosities, black with the dye
Of falsehood, to deceive the masses and
To breed dissension in our peaceful land.

But even in enlightened times, we've seen
Wise men and gentle women to have been
Burned at the stake, because, like Faustus, they
Were deemed possessed of demons. And to-day,
'Neath hydra-headed Abolition's sway,
If license, such as Cotton Mather's time
Permitted, granted was—the knell would chime
For each slaveholder, and his whitening bones
Would bleach on cold fanaticism's stones,
The while his blistering flesh would writhe and
      broil
On Black Republican gridirons!
                              What turmoil
A band of malcontents can ever raise,
Even while they cover it with prayer and praise—
Thus desecrating true religion's robe,
While rancorous wounds with malice dire they
      probe,
Until the festering sores spread far and near,
And purity itself may almost fear
To catch the infection. But we still will hope
Right-judging minds exist in the broad scope
Our Northern limits have, and they will yet
A better influence bring to bear, and set

The index on the dial's face to show
Their erring brothers the right road to go,
Nor let our country's name become a jest,
For scoffing nations to make manifest;
Our flag dishonored, and our unity
A by-word in each broad community!
For all must see (unless willfully blind)
How useless 't is to hope, the South to bind
With fetters, or to think she'll yield to those
Whom she regards as bitterest of foes;
Give up her lawful rights, which soul and sense
At present sanction, to the vain pretense
Of sympathy and pure philanthropy
That's urged by madness or misanthropy,
And seeks to do an evil to a race,
Who in creation's aim hold the right place
In the progressive scale of being.
                                        What

But sheer infatuation, e'er could plot
So wild a scheme as it would prove to be,
If e'er effected, all our Blacks to free?
Why, such a gang of paupers, or, still worse,
Of thieves and villains, would our country curse,
That even Europe's gipsy hordes could not

Compare with; for the Negro is a sot
Of beastial description, and when free
Spends most his time in low debauchery.
And this the population that would spread,
In vagrant swarms, and in their vileness, shed
A merited opprobium on the head
That first conceived the - wondrous plan that
      set
The ball in motion!

                          O! loose not the jet
Of the dark fountain whose rank, muddy flow,
Would stain our land's unblemished, spotless
      snow,
And where fair Peace and Plenty reign, send
      Want
With haggard brow, shrunk limbs, and visage
      gaunt.
  The eighty-first year of our freedom crashed
Like a huge bomb-shell o'er the world! War
      clash'd
Its tocsin o'er the Eastern Hemisphere.
For scarce did gentle Peace descend to bear
Her olive-leaf across the Black Sea's wave,
When India burst her prison doors and gave

Dread prestige of her barbarous strength and
    might,
Her vengeance dire with bloody pen to write!
The footfalls of advancing liberty
Echoed thro' Spain and sunny Italy,
Startling the powers that be—all Europe felt
That thrones and monarchies were doomed to
    melt
In the pure crucible of Justice. Still
The gold must first be tried, its strength must fill
The measure of endurance, ere the pure
Metal may from the dross be drained—we're sure
By all analogy, that man must be
First fitted for it, ere he can be free!
On our own continent went, hand in hand,
Revolting states. Again that fated land,
Uneasy Mexico, made other laws
Without advancing her unhappy cause
A single step toward better government
Or national prosperity. There went
Thro' Central America, the clash
Of civil war, and, twice, the meteor flash
Of baseless government. Republics, too,
In South America, gave proofs anew

Of instability, by popular
Disturbances; and everywhere the car
Of warfare national, rolled with its stains
Of blood, its kindred throes and gnawing pains;
Save in our own Republic's peaceful shade,
Which Heaven forbid it ever shall invade;
For rather than our banner shall be rent
And on the wild gale of disunion sent
To furnish vultures' nests; or tattered, wave
Above our Constitution's early grave;
I would exclaim, as did a noble one
Of nature's freemen, and the patriot son
Who sought his own loved but down-trodden land
To save from despotism's iron band:
"May all the colors of God's bow be torn
Asunder ere that banner's stripes!"

The worn

And weary footsteps of the warring past
With blood have made their deep-set marks, and
    cast
Their warnings forth upon the gale, to show
The tide of liberty is in its flow;
And tho' the ebb may come, 't will swell anew
And rise to higher hights when full and true

The rounding moon of Progress shall have filled
Her horns, and o'er the purity distilled
From the foul lees of despotism's night,
Shines out with ripe perfection's glowing light
To gild each billow, silver-crest each wave
Of wrong or violence, and thro' the cave
Where Lethe's waters wash remembrance out;
Turn every stream of discord, dread, and doubt,
To be but things forgotten. Ah! ere then,
How many changes shall be wrought 'mong
    men,
And fallacies, and feuds, and creeds give way,
Ere on the horizon the perfect day
Shall gleam, when peace and concord sweet shall
    bind
The world's great family of human kind!
  My Country! 'twas *thy* priceless boon to lead
The way to better things, nor do I need
The prophet's mantle to descend on me
To tell how glorious may thy future be
Among the nations of the earth, if thou
But crush fanaticism. Thorns will grow
On fairest roses, but their points we see,
And by destroying, may not wounded be.

Why should we prostitute our better sense
By granting license to each foul pretense
That cloaks the wish for undisputed power
'Neath cover of religion's holy dower,
And throws contempt on laws and government,
Which to establish our forefathers went
Thro' seas of blood, and battles' groans and
    shrieks?
Must *we* now yield to mad dictation's freaks,
And tamely suffer domination's rules,
Which were but made, at best, to fetter fools?
  O! for the eloquence that thrilled upon
The heart-strings of his countrymen, when on
The forum bold Virginia's son stood forth,
And, one by one, let fall the pearls whose worth
A nation now attests. Ah! one might give
Their heart's blood, drop by drop, if they could
    live
One glorious hour like that that lighted on
The brow of Patrick Henry when he won
The Assembly's ear, and pointed to the course
To guide his country's bark thro' breakers worse
Than helmsman other than a hero e'er
Would fearless dash thro', and full boldly steer

Upon the bristling rock of war's fierce front.
O! for a draught from the celestial fount
Of inspiration, that my pen might trace
The lineaments of Truth's all-perfect face,
To show my brethren, by the contrast, how
Ungainly and uncouth foul Error's brow—
That they may thereby her embraces flee,
And shake the incubus of bigotry
From their half-paralyzed perceptions!

                              Then

Our star, whose light is dimming fast 'mong men,
Would burst the clouds by traitors raised, and
    shine
Fair as yon hosts in galaxy divine!
An ambient ray to gild our mighty deeds;
A holy flame unswerved by feuds or creeds;
The torch whereby oppression sees the way
To flee from darkness unto bright noonday;
The Vestal's lamp, by purity supplied,
That quenchless blazes over time and tide!

    Alas! that e'er our honored name should be
Coupled with such rank, factious anarchy
As 'tis to-day! Must our broad land be riven
With broils, because it is the will of Heaven

12

To make it the blest means a class to save
From Heathenism's dark, polluted grave?
Forbid it, Justice! God of Power and Might!
Roll back the scroll of ignorance—let light
From thy eternal hills shower knowledge down:
And take thou from our country's brow the crown
Of thorns that's rankling, festering there!
O, Father! hear an earnest, fervent prayer.
   'Tis not to pettifogging dogmatists
I would appeal—as well hope thro' thick mists
To steer in safety, as that one of those
Unyielding wranglers who the South oppose,
Should list *my* feeble voice—but to " good men
And true," I'd show, *their* honor's questioned,
    when
By weak supineness they encourage those
Whose conduct proves them but their country's
    foes,
And silently look on to see the rights
Of freemen trampled by those buckram knights,
Who using Sambo for their dastard shield,
Take a bold stand in policy's sham field,
And fain would pass for pure philanthropists
At the expense of all wherein consists

Faith with their fellow-man ! O ! brothers, why—
Ye who can boast a truth-discerning eye—
Why will ye suffer this foul leprosy
To stain your better nature? Ye might be
The means, if you'd exert the slumbering power
That God has vested in you, this black hour
To blot from out the calendar—nor let
Our country be the sacrifice which yet
Unto this Moloch must be offered, and
Which will another Tophet make our land.

    That land, by heroes' blood redeemed, made
      pure,
The open-armed and ever friendly shore
That welcomes all who seek its peaceful strand—
That *it* should groan beneath the scorching brand
Placed by its children on its manhood's brow!
That *they*, of *all*, should question the pure vow
Baptized in blood, but registered in praise
Beneath the dawn that's brought us these blest
      days
Of plenty and prosperity ! O ! shame
On all who let a dastard purpose, lame
In the poor arguments with which it boasts
Of strength—cover their eyes to hosts

Of blessings which the very law that they
Contend against, brings to us all to-day !
Yes, *all !* for who dare say the Black is not
Far happier, and far better in his lot
('Tho' it be groaned o'er by each sycophant
Whose whole religion's humbugging and cant),
Of a well treated and much-cared-for slave,
Than in a state of freedom left to brave
Not only outside wants and penury,
But *his own savage nature's tenure?*   He
Has in himself a greater foe than e'er
He'd find in a kind master's thoughtful care,
Tho' would-be friends seek to divest him of
His blessings, showing thereby neither love
Nor kindness prompts their measures, but desire
For domination kindles the wild fire
To whose red, hissing flames their brethren's
     rights
Are recklessly consigned.

                          My pen indites
These truths, not that I would decry the North—
I state but simple facts for what they're worth—
For *all* this land my country is, and wrong
Or right, is still MY NATIVE LAND !   O ! strong

The ties forged by those magic words, to bind
The human heart, to link it to its kind;
And dastard he who'd seek to set a stain
Upon the sod that gave him birth, or gain
A doubtful reputation at the shrine
That immolates all that is most divine
Or sacred held by man! Not this, not this
The paltry motive whose base prompting is
The lever which calls forth what I indite;
But when a people willfully invite
Contention, as the Northern mass has done
By heaping slanders and abuse upon
That section of our land known as " The South,"
And using for this means the ready mouth
Of pulpit, press, and rostrum, to create
A furore false 'gainst each slaveholding State—
It is but natural that this should cause
Some refutation of our outraged laws
To be attempted; tho' the arm that wields
The defensive armor, boasts not manhood's shields
Of confidence and liberty of speech;
Yet once, *a little child was brought to teach*
Wise men, and sat down in their midst!
And 't is this simple thought aroused, that bids

Me lift my feeble voice to quell the storm,
And call on God to aid the motive warm
And sincere, that from my heart of hearts
Leaps into words, and its own strength imparts
To what my pen, without that motive true,
Could never fashion or do justice to.

   Believe it, brothers, I but seek to bind
Our fearfully disjointed causes, twined
Like the soft tendrils of a clinging vine
Around one parent tree—yet mine, and thine,
'Stead of converging toward blest unity,
Spread, as the poles, asunder! This may be
The wild chimera of an enthusiast's brain—
But yet I'll hope, that, like the spring's soft
    rain,
My admonitions may fall on good seeds
To yield an hundred fold, our country's needs
Full bounteously to furnish and supply
With wholesome food, fair to the polished eye
Of taste, and also palatable to
The healthy throat of probity.

                 And now,
That matter settled—I would simply ask,
Why do our Northern brethren take the task,

The odious task, upon themselves to pry
Into our business, and to decry
Our institutions and our systems, all,
Domestic, civil, and political?
Have Southerners this course pursued toward
    theirs?
Or ever sowed detraction's spreading tares
To choke the growth of sympathy abroad,
And by base slanders, half unsheath the sword
Of popular opinion in *their* face?
They, who with us, should in the struggling race
Of excellence go side by side, nor let
A paltry matter of opinion set
Wide open the broad floodgates of the tide
That sweeps our common interests thus wide
Apart. Not such the holy chain that wound
With adamantine links our nation round,
When those brave hearts, with firm reliance on
Divine protection in their union,
Mutually to each other pledged their lives,
Their fortunes, and their sacred honor!

> Strives
There one, of all the wrangling demagogues,
Whose leaden weight our native progress clogs,

To benefit his country, or impart
New impetus to college, church, or mart?
Say, rather, is not selfish interest
And personal aggrandizement, at the best,
The prompting motives for each fierce assault
That even at falsehood's barrier does not halt,
But leaps alike o'er friend and foe, to gain
The dizzy hights of power, tho' bought with
    pain?

   Ah! would impartial eyes but only ope,
Survey our rights and wrongs in widest scope,
Compare our institutions and our laws,
And make our grievances a common cause;
Then, with the wand of justice, mete to all
An *equal* footing in our Congress Hall;
Nor let dictation mount its hobby there,
And set its iron heel on all that's fair,
Or equitable to a portion of
The people—meeting their demands with scoff,
Or covering with deceitful smile, a dread
And treacherous purpose, to lay low the head
That shrunk not when its country called to save
Sweet heaven-born Liberty from the dark grave
Dug by oppression; but stood bravely forth

With form erect, firm heart, and steadfast worth,
Pledged to the death to fight for rights which now
By brethren's hands are wrenched from its own
    brow. ‹

   This agitated question—Slavery—
Has called forth more bombastic bravery,
And more inflated Furiosos brought
Forth from oblivion's somber, dingy court,
To war in rhetoric's windy field, than e'er
Fanaticism did before. And here
I 'll digress, just to tell you why 't is so:
Didst ever note how prone are all below,
To *add* to what they hear? Just like the crow
Tradition—where a man gave out that he
Did something vomit, black as crow could be;
When this had gone the village circuit round,
The swiftly-rolling ball had swelled, 't was found,
To such a size, that it was clearly shown
He 'd thrown up *three black crows!*

                 I freely own
The joke is rather stale, but not less true
To human nature's foibles, which with new
Adornments dress each story, foul or just,
And mountains make out of each grain of dust;

  13

And there are never wanting idlers, who
Will roll the atom till each layer anew
Vests with increasing strength the gaining ball;
Then, as a mighty avalanche, its fall
Awakens sleeping echoes far and near
And crushes all who come within its sphere!
    And so, each idle tale that floated thro'
The regions of "free soil," black crow like,
    drew
Its idle followers to roll the ball
E 'en to the portals of our Congress Hall,
Where now, a threatened avalanche, it swings
Upon a single thread—and discord brings
O'er our fair land, whose rulers scarcely know
How Abolition's tongue can turn a crow
To a huge condor—just as malice can
Grind to a pigmy a true-hearted man!
    What makes the matter worse (but this is
    still
Only a like sad phase of human ill),
These all-wise boasters who decry the South,
Have gained their knowledge only by the mouth
Of Rumor—she of many tongues—the foul
Base slanderer, whose harsh, discordant howl

Grates on the ear of sensibility,
And shocks the virtuous to the last degree,
But who is welcomed by her colleagues dear
With shouts of joy and cries of Hear! hear!
    hear!
They 've never sought to sift the chaff to find
The grains of truth, but rashly have combined
To crush the South, because her foes see fit
To clamor loud, and ceaseless strive for it.
    Come with me, one and all, unto this land
I 'll lead you gently, with a loving hand,
And point out all its beauties, if I can,
Until, for very shame, you 'll to a man
Exclaim : " Is this the people, these the laws
We 've sought to crush ? O ! surely, we must
    pause
In our mad judgment of an upright cause
That wide disseminates its blessings, and
With peace and plenty crowns a happy land,
Where each the station holds by Providence
Assigned him—and where broad diverging
    thence
The bounteous streams of industry glide on
To beautify our common country."

Gone
Will be all prejudice, if with the eye
Of truth you seek our merits to descry,
And, with the tongue of probity, send forth
Your firm convictions for just what they 're worth,
When you have fairly weighed us and our cause
'Gainst wild fanaticism's fickle laws.

The South.

WHERE the fair tropic's golden fruits expand
Beneath the day god's glances, smiles a land
Of roses—'t is fair Flora's vast parterre
She holds her court and highest revels there,
Where clustering multiflorous buds half blown,
O'ercanopy her queenly dahlia throne ;
And blue-eyed violets kiss her dainty feet
As up the dewy lawn they twinkle fleet ;
And waxen lilies shade their soft cheeks pale,
And o'er their loveliness draw snowy vail
As the gay goddess passes with her train,
These garden nuns who pageantry hold vain !
Here, too, those sycophants of flowerdom
That cling and cringe to each and all that come,
Convolvuluses, decked in garments gay,
Are born to live and die in one short day
(The doom of vanity)! And here is one,
The gentle heliotrope, that to the sun

Doth constant turn in adoration still
Where'er he moves, the guider of her will—
Who, seeking not to charm, charms all the
    more;
For unobtrusive merit's ever sure
To win its way among the just and good
Where arrogance will fail!
                  ·Beneath a hood
Of rose-color or purest white, you spy
The periwinkle's watching, yellow eye,
With envy glaring at the lovely rose,
Whose blushes deepen as her lips unclose
To breathe a welcome to the humming-bird
That's whispering in her ear the witching word
With which he 's wiled full many a gentle flower;
Then left, to wander in a fresher bower,
When he has rifled it of all its sweets.
Here, too, transformed Adonis faithful greets
The realms of air, as 't is his right to be
Known half the year as gay anemone,
Flower of the wind, and earliest of the spring,
To tell of coming buds and blossoming.
The purple orchis waves in wildness here;
And sweet forget-me-nots, like faith, appear

With starry eyes that smile and seem to say,
Love can abide fell sorrow's darkest day
If nourished by fidelity—and what
But this thy emblem, blest forget-me-not?

Thus, everywhere around the fairies write
Their loving messages, their deeds indite—
You see their rings beneath the myrtle's boughs,
The whispering pines but echo their soft vows,
And many a creamy white magnolia leaf
Shows creases where they've written sonnets brief;
And grave old oaks shake their gray mossy hairs,
While in the moonlight dance the elfin pairs
To the sweet south wind's music, stealing o'er
Some silvery lake's enameled shelly shore;
Or sighing thro' some fragrant orange grove
Where mocking-birds discourse melodious love,
And starry watchers in the blue afar
Wink their bright eyes as swells each trilling bar
To blend with heaven's seraphic melodies
As softly as the dew falls on the seas—
A half-tone in the harmony of spheres,
But swelling still the choral chant of years,
As up the sounding aisles of space it rolls
To echo thro' the realms of happy souls!

Here, too, Pomona scatters graciously
Her luscious favors, and Vertumnus (he,
Her youthful spouse) his horn of plenty, here
Replenishes throughout the changing year;
While Ceres blesses all the fruitful land,
And bids it yield its sweets at her command;
And grateful thousands lift their voices high
In songs of joy that echo to the sky,
And freely use the blessings love has given.
  By *using*—not abusing—'t is to Heaven
Mankind returneth thanks, and earth can raise
A "new song" to the great Creator's praise
For all his wondrous gifts.   "Let everything
That hath breath praise the Lord!"—we 're taught
        to sing
By the great Psalmist; and we glorify
Him   in   his   works   when   'neath   his   arching
    sky
We reap the harvest of his providence.
Be sure he has not sent his bounties hence
To lead us into temptation, without still
Our minds impressing with the woful ill
That follows all abuses—and the wise
Can see the medium with truth's loving eyes,

And all enjoy; but know where lies the mark
Which to o'erstep turns every light to dark;
Yet in its moderate limits circles all
Of harmless pleasure on this earthly ball,
And in its innocent enjoyment gives
A sounding "song of praise" from each that lives!
   'T is here that *true* religion really reigns—
For God's great laws progress without the stains
That Error's worshipers imprint—the schisms
Wrought by false prophets, with their "ists" and
    "isms;"
Those stumbling-blocks which clog the road of faith
To trip the weak, whose end is moral death.
No—thanks to an all-wise, protecting Power,
That's guided us aright unto this hour,
And from all evil safe delivered us—
Our eyes of truth can see the incubus
That holds with demon strength the fast-closed lids
Of all fanaticism's hosts, and bids
Calm Reason yield her throne while Error sits
In judgment on the rights of man.
                Cry "quits,"
Ye schemers wild! come to our land and learn
Of those, whose laws ye in your ignorance spurn;

That 'tis consistent with benevolence
And one of the designs of Providence,
To put each thing, or creature to its use—
(Neglect's as great a sin as is abuse)—
And surely God designed that each should fill
A relative position, that would still
Go to complete a yet perfecting whole
Whence comfort, welfare, happiness will roll
To circle man and beautify the earth
Thro' its own creatures of progressive birth.

And here that law works in its widest sense,
And shows in its results, the vain pretense
That's urged by wrangling abolitionism,
That there exists a fierce antagonism
Between the Black and White man. 'Tis not so
When in their *true relation*, each can go
In harmony along the upward scale;
But discord rises when rude hands assail
The heaven-strung instrument, and seek to place
Among fine treble chords the harsher base.
And thus the social lyre is out of tune,
When, as co-equals, Negroes can commune
With White men; for they are not fit to be
Left their own masters, self-dependent, free!

As well let loose your ox, your horse, your cow,
And then expect that one will to the plow
Back of his own accord—the other leap
Into harness—and old Brindle keep
True to her trust, and seek the dairy's door—
As that a liberated Black will pour
His labor forth for hire!
     And so, we see,
The Negro race can only useful be
By working in a rank subordinate
To greater intellect; and thus the great
Design of an all-wise Creator is
Fulfilled, by giving each his place in this
Progressing, fruitful world, which man must till
To cause it yield abundantly, to fill
His measure full to overflowing, and
With plenteousness to crown a happy land.
 Tho' nature has done much, man must do
  more
Of this, experience makes us very sure;
And if the South would firmly keep the trust
Reposed in her by One both true and just,
She'll go unflinching on her steady course,
And let wild Faction scream .till it grows hoarse,

And prove herself her country's truest friend
In thus maintaining laws which in the end
Will work their own redemption—for they give
The real principles to truly live
E'en to that class that's groaned over as slaves
In rescuing them from their living graves
Of barbarism, and developing
Their attributes.   There's nothing else will bring
The negro race within the social ring,
To yield their resources of labor here,
Without we place them in their proper sphere.
    That is a morbid, false philanthropy,
The offspring of a weak misanthropy,
That bids us loosen o'er our thriving lands
Paupers and thieves where now are happy bands
Of disciplined and well-conducted slaves.
'T is madness or sheer wantonness thus raves;
As neither Black or White man thus could be
A beneficiary in the least degree.
For one would sink to beastial indolence,
The other lack the means of self-defense
Against privation's biting stings; for he
Is not by constitution made to be
Exposed to ardent heat like him whose birth

Spontaneous was with torrid climes of earth.
And all these fertile, beauteous lands would lie
Uncultivated 'neath a burning sky;
The main commodity that gives, we know,
Employment to thousands here below
That swells the tithes of commerce, and that fills
The revenues of other States—distills
Its benefits North, South, East, West, to all—
Would fail, for want of force to swing the ball
That bids the manufacturing levers work,
And feeds the very mouths that twist and jerk
While basely leveling reproof at those
Who 've proved their greatest friends instead of
    foes.
    Let but slave labor in the cotton field
Come to an end, and where will be the yield
That Northern factors pocket? Ah! be sure
The wolf will be not only at *our* door,
But *all* our country will cry out, too late,
When small receipts of customs show that hate
Has crushed the means that gave us our in-
    crease,
And brought contentious strife where all was
    peace.

God's purposes in all things are subserved—
His will has still controlled, and never swerved,
Since mingling elements their march began
In circling changes till they fashioned man,
Who, with his mortal eyes, may fail to see
The slow, mysterious ways of Deity.
But he may rest assured they 're good and just;
And so, with childlike confidence and trust,
Abide His time, who in the beginning gave
To time its limits, and prepared the grave
In which old things shall sink into decay,
When progress shall have reached the brighter
    day
To which convergent from creation's morn
All things terrestrial have been upward drawn
By cords of love—fulfilling the design
Eternal, glorious, infinite, divine !

Man may not hasten the Almighty's hand,
That rules the storm or sways the breezes bland—
That opes the gates of Death, and parts the
    way
For light to enter thro' the realms of day—
That scattereth the east wind o'er the earth,
And gave each shining star its glorious birth !

He may not question the Eternal One,
Who from the whirlwind spake to that poor
    son
Of sorrow, when he mourned his hapless fate—
To show him, that 't is God alone is great.
And man must still submit to his decrees;
He, who the influences of Pleiades
Can bind, or loose Orion's bands—can guide
Arcturus with his sons, o'er the blue tide
Of space—or, in his season, can bring forth
Mazzaroth!
           We're taught by this, the worth
Of patiently submitting to God's will,
Which in the end will prove his wondrous skill
By turning wrong to right, and guiding all
Conditions on this ever-moving ball,
So that their destined ends, perfected, may
Add brighter glories to the coming day,
Which, struggling with the darkness, seeks to
    climb
The distant zenith o'er the hights of time,
And shed o'er earth refulgent light sublime.
    Why will the North submit to be the tool
Of monarchists, who seek a world-wide rule,

And labor without ceasing, early, late,
Our institutions to exterminate?
And to this end dogmatically strive,
By blowing a faint spark until, a live
And glowing coal, it threatens all the land
To turn to a fierce, quivering, flaming brand,
Which, if not checked, will hissingly burn on
Until it melts our bands of union,
And leaves the altar of our liberty,
A charred and blackened ruin!

                           This, we see,
Is but the aim of those who've duped the
    North,
By propagating doctrines whose whole worth
Lay in the selfish end to be attained.
And well they've labored, and their end's near
    gained;
Those antislavery demagogues, with seed
Plucked from the Old World's crown and scepter
    breed,
Which they have planted in our Northern soil,
And pruned and watered, till their ceaseless toil
Has been rewarded—for their dupes and tools
Strive with them now to overturn the rules

Laid down by their forefathers, lend their strength
To curtail freemen's rights, by breadth and length;
Nor would they shrink to strike the dastard blow
E'en if their country's head was thus laid low!
  Why urge the dogma of equality?
The White and Black can never equal be!
God ne'er designed it, else we had not seen
Their attributes so different to have been.
And even the poor Indians now own
This to be true—as it is clearly shown
In the late delegations of some tribes
Of red men to our government. The scribes
On that occasion, penned things trite and true,
Altho' 't was untaught tongues gave utterance to
The maxims wise—'t was Nature speaking thro'
Her forest-children's lips. Hear what she said:
  " My Grandfather ! " spoke one of the chiefs,
    red,
Addressing the Great Ruler of our land;
" This land on which to-day you firmly stand,
Belonged to me. 'T was the Great Spirit's will
That you should take it from us! " Speaking still
He added: " *The Great Spirit! that made you*
More powerful than me, was partial to

You, and a better color gave than me ;
For it was the Great Spirit's will that we
Both came into existence. You 're a man,
My Grandfather, and so am I."

                              Say, can
Our vaunted wisdom and enlightenment
Lead us to wiser issues, than the bent
Of observation in rude savage breast
Which judges causes by results ?   The test
In this case, was the White man's power
Which triumphed o'er the Indian's given hour,
And proved to this poor forest child, how vast
The line of demarcation that is cast
Between the races; that the weaker, still
Must follow guidance from superior skill,
If they would find the road from wrong to right
And merge from darkness into broad noon-light.
   How, then, we ask each antislaveryite,
Are we to guide the African aright?
We ne'er can hope that land to colonize;
At least, the way's not clear *yet* to our eyes,
Tho' nothing is impossible with God !
And should the time arrive,· he 'll point the
   road.

But for the present, we but follow his
Appointments, when we give a place to this
Poor savage in our midst, and kindly try
To open his long-closed, benighted eye
To better things—the while we may not place
His guidance in his own hands, for the race
Would run to ruin faster than the mass
Of dingy Black Republicans now pass;
But, as we'd train a little child to go
Where wisdom pointed us to guide it so,
Yet hold the leading-string to check, whene'er
It deviated from a proper sphere,
So, with this simple child of savage birth,
We seek to point his steps aright on earth,
Supply his wants by turning his own strength
In proper channels, where 't will yield at length
Not only personal necessities,
But all mankind will, also, in degrees
Be the recipients of the warming stream
Of light, that glides from well-directed beam,
Which else, obscured beneath a thick vail, dark
Would lie, because the bright Promethean spark
Of *true* philanthropy, was quenched by hate
That spat upon its mission pure and great!

Why is the South denied equality
Within the Union? She does not, we see,
Ask anything unjust, unwise, untrue
To the great cause which led her to imbrue
With her heart's blood the standard of our
    land
To free it from oppression's galling band !
Is it forgotten how her gallant sons
Risked life and fortune for us favored ones
That are the beneficiaries ? Say,
Had Thomas Jefferson lived in our day
To see the cause for which he labored long,
Early and late—attacked thus by a strong,
Hot-headed host of fanatics, whose ire
Was kindled at a foreign kingdom's fire,
To be the means of ruining that cause
Which dared oppose the Old World's grinding
    laws—
How would his pure, unselfish spirit shrink
To see his country trembling on the brink
Of the deep chasm dug by envy here
To gulf this hated Western hemisphere
Before its herald star shall lead all on
To follow in the path thus nobly gone

So far; to crush it ere its rays divine
Shall draw all earth to worship at the shrine
Of Liberty—that dragon to the breed
Of despots, who would shout to see it bleed,
And now are laughing in their sleeves, to see
What dupes they've made among the enemy;
And how New England (spite of boasted wit)
Holds her blind side for them the coat to fit,
Remodel the lean wearer, puff, and pad
To suit monarchial dogmas.
                                    'Tis too bad,
That wrong directed sympathy should lead
To the commission of so foul a deed
As will be perpetrated if the rights
Of the fair South are subject to such slights
As have been heaped upon it, far and wide,
Where'er has flowed the muddy, surging tide
Of Abolition. Yes, a deed so foul
That angels well may weep at—demons howl—
When our fair Union is rent in twain,
As it *must be*, if this upheaving main
Is suffered longer to encroach upon
Our borders. It has swelled and rolled still
    on,

Bearing upon its chafing waves the scum
Of party feeling, till the drift's become
A formidable barrier which shuts in
Our privileges ; and the angry din
Of battle, embryoed in words at first,
Will yet upon our startled hearing burst
If longer parley is allowed.

                    " Thus far,
And no farther shalt thou go," is just ; a bar
Must ever stop oppression, let it come
From any source it will, e'en from our home.
We may regret the dire necessity
That forces the sad deed ; but we must be
Placed in our *true* position in this land,
And then we 'll pledge our lives to nobly stand
By it, as we have ever done, thro' good
Or ill. But if the prating, meddling brood
Of Black Republicans must dictate to
Our government, and show it what to do ;
And Southern rights, equality, and space
Be left for these foul demagogues to trace
The limits of—then must we look to God
To judge our cause, and use the avenging
     rod,

If we do err in seeking for ourselves
A standard for which justice vainly delves
At present!
           Vail thy face, fair Liberty!
If this, thy boasted throne, is thus to be
Ruled by rank faction. 'Tis a misnomer,
Might well incite satiric caviler
To call it thy abiding place, or raise
Thy altar, if we desecrate thy praise
In this way; if the mob can sway the mass,
And trample common sense, to rudely pass
Beyond all barriers social, civil, and
Implant their right to lead and rule the land—
Dictate to and chastise, control and teach,
Let hatred prompt, fanaticism preach,
And Idiocy condemn, approve, or boast
With maudlin leer, that *it* can rule the roast!
That individual sovereignty must yield
When cap-and-bells and long-ears take the
    field
To bray down justice and equality
With venomed partisan garrulity.
  We'll now take up the term "equality,"
The Abolition watchword! First, we see,

The lexicographer defining it
As " uniformity," an equal fit
Of two or more things to each other.   See,
If by this rule, the White and Black can be
On the same footing?   And, again, we find
The word as " similarity," defined.
Pray, will you *equalizers* tell us, where,
Or in what manner, habit, Negroes are
Or ever can be, similar to Whites ?
The question all your logic now invites.
Come one and all, with Freddy at your head,
Here's chance for screaming, if you wish to shed
A light on this *dark* subject; for I own
I've tried to fathom it, but fairly shown
My inability to do so.   Now,
I call on *you* to speak—no matter how—
We'll make excuses for your want of grace,
In Balaam's time a like event took place!
We only ask you to enlighten us,
Upon a point that you so oft discuss,
That we may share your erudition, and
Be blest partakers of its precepts grand,
Which in the rules of order, " Heaven's first law,"
Can find an error and detect a flaw

And (wiser than Omnipotence) aspire
To re-string all the chords of Nature's lyre,
So that the squeaking fiddle of base peers
May drown the rolling anthems of the spheres!
    Meantime, I'll tell you how the South defines
Equality: We've seen, each star that shines
With phosphorescent gleam in ether's sea,
Hath in itself a differing degree
Of glory—a fixed light assigned each one.
We're told, "There is a glory of the sun,
Another of the moon, and of the stars,
And one star differs from another." Wars
There any 'gainst this creed? Then let him look
Above, in the blue-covered, gilded book,
Whose leaves are ever open to his sight,
And read the lesson God's pen there did write
For man to profit by. He'll learn to know
That *true* equality, above, below,
Consists in *each thing holding its own place;*
Whether a system, world, or but a race,
If its light shine in its own given sphere,
It radiates a beam both bright and clear,
Tho' but a planet borrowing its rays
From golden sun glowing with inward blaze.
    15

But O! how vain to hope to emulate
The flooded splendor of its primary great;
To equal the bright source of its own light!
Then its dependence would soon come to sight.
The only equalizing process is
Its own true orbit to hold fast in this
Grand panorama, still to add its mite
Of usefulness, and shed its borrowed light,
The universe to bless; and then 't will be
Equal to suns of radiant degree!
And such alone is true equality,
To do your duty in that station God
Hath here appointed, by his wondrous word.
Let man do this—angels can do no more—
If he would equal those who rapt adore
Their Great Creator, face to face, where rolls
The sounding praises of enfranchised souls!

Where is the Negro's field of usefulness?
Is it in council-chamber, at the press,
Or bar; in pulpit, auditorium,
Or learning's intricate emporium?
Say, can he climb Parnassus, or entwine
The laurel plucked where roam the Heavenly
    Nine?

Has Deity imprinted on his brow
The seal to which all creatures humbly bow?
Do pearls of thought there scintillate and gleam,
Or rich imaginings send forth a stream
Of living glory's radiating beam?
　You may reply, The pearls want polishing;
How test their rays, if ne'er abolishing
Their rough crustations? Ah! true gems will show
Themselves, even if bedded far below
Their outer coverings; so may we find
In the uneducated, gleams of mind,
Which 'neath the mental lapidary's hand
May luster get to fit them to command!
But we apply the lens in vain, in vain
To find such rays within the Negro's brain—
For there alone the coarser instincts reign.
Refinement, elegance, or perfect taste,
If planted there, would surely run to waste;
The soil is uncongenial to such growth—
Imagination and reflection both
Are wanting; but the animal, combined
With the domestic properties, is shrined
Which gives the Negro a subordinate
Relation to the White man. 'T is his fate—

The fiat of creation—that he still
This rank below must uncomplaining fill.
To place him on the White man's level, we
Destroy the basis of equality—
We're only equal in our proper spheres!
But to annul this footing now appears
To be the end and aim of those who strive,
Against all principle, to keep alive
The quivering flame, lit in unholy cause
Against creation's and our Maker's laws!

   This shows, the fundamental principles
Of what knaves vaunt about in madd'ning yells,
So far exceed their gross perceptions, that
In Truth's pure light, they're blind as is a bat
In sunshine!   So they spout, and rant, and rave
Bombastic'ly about the Southern Slave
(Who'd open wide his eyes to hear them tell
How cruelly he's treated); and they swell
His grievances to such a blackened stream
That Styx compared to it, would fairly gleam
With lacteal luster.   They dark portraits draw
In falsehood's hues, of sanguine conflicts raw,
Between psalm-singing Uncle Toms, and Turks
Of masters fierce—(and, by the way, there lurks

A clue to the enlightenment of one
Dark labyrinth in a sheer romance, but done
To suit a morbid appetite. We find,
The coarse, harsh master, Mistress Stowe has
    shrin'd
To represent a *Southern Planter*, claims
New England as his birthplace! Hot, would
    shame's
Bright blood mount flaming to the cheeks and
    brows
Of the South's own true-hearted sons, if vows
Of cruelty and deeds of blood should be
E'er dreamed of *by them*, such as one " Legree"
Is made the mover of in that tirade.
But he but follows all his colleagues' trade—
Dictation to the death, is their employ?
And this is why they pour their base alloy
O'er our pure laws, and prate equality
While crushing it with iron heel.)
                      We see
How far fanaticism leads men on,
By measuring the lengths these dupes have gone;
Who, all-forgetful of the ties that bind
These States in union, by joint interest twined,

Would take from us, their equals by God's laws,
A right to judge or advocate a cause
Involving national prosperity,
And circumscribe in limited degree
Our territory, while they dwarf, confine
Our resources in bigotry's dark mine;
As may be seen by all who look abroad
And view the flaming, bright despotic sword
Of Empire, which the North's cold hand now waits
To grasp, ere fiercely it decapitates
That gorgon in its path—the sunny South—
Who, let her but essay to ope her mouth,
Her wholesome precepts are transformed to snakes
By those who in Power's temple hold the stakes,
And fearful of our Federal rights and rules,
Remodel them to suit despotic schools!

Your philanthropic novel writers may
Work on credulity, and mayhap, sway
The tender-hearted for a time, with scenes
Drawn from imagination's painted screens,
And highly colored to comport with what
Their colleagues wildly scheme and basely plot
'Gainst every argument of common sense,
To give a substance to a false pretense,

And hoodwink justice, while they seek to gain
The balance of that power for which they strain
Each nerve and every fiber of heart, soul, sense,
Aided by rank duplicity; and hence
They work their way where honest folk draw
    back,
Preferring the straightforward, open track,
Open alike to friend and foe, that all
May see their movements, if they rise or fall,
Disdaining subterfuge, and seeking still
To call forth friendliness and pure good-will
From their opponents; but, in case they fail,
Ready to boldly guard what foes assail,
Stand by their rights, as freemen should, to death,
And die proclaiming them with latest breath,
If need be!
           This, the difference, that lies
Open to all impartial, candid eyes,
Between the North and South to-day. The land,
Purchased with price of blood by patriot band,
Made the low theater of party strife.
But, thanks to God! the South drew not the knife
Upon her brother's heart; her work and cares
Have ever been about her own affairs,

With faith in all her kindred, North, East, West,
She's wisely thought they knew their business
    best,
And were as capable of minding it
As she would be to leave her own and sit
In judgment on their actions. *All* can find
Sufficient business of their own to mind,
Without a thankless interference in
The affairs of others. Thus, the deep sin
Of severing the bonds left to us pure,
If perpetrated, lies not at our door.
We've ever been true to the sacred cause
Which led our forefathers to fight for laws
Which would secure them from oppression—*now*
We feel that hot brand scaring our own brow,
And 't is a brother's hand hath placed it there!
We pause—for *him* to move it—ere we tear
It ruthlessly from the proud head it thus
Dishonors!
       Dear the Union is to us—
Dear from its history, and from the names
Enrolled upon its archives! Ne'er will shame's
Condemning flush rise on the South's fair face
When called her moiety therein to trace.

She sent her Washington to lead the host
To freedom ! and may, all-exultant, boast
Another noble star of first degree,
The true apostle of sweet Liberty,
In Thomas Jefferson, the wise, the good !
And in her glorious galaxy there stood
Conspicuous, Henry, Morgan, Marion.
Shall names like these fail to shine out upon
Her honor, and to increase its light ? And still
Are hosts of others every blank to fill ;
There, Shelby, Laurens, Pinckney, Sumter, tell
That patriot hearts in Southern bosoms dwell ;
And Eutaw's field, and Yorktown's battered walls,
Show courage is not wanting when the calls
Of country ask avenging arms to save
From tyranny's dishonored, darksome grave.
Proud Tarleton's lowered crest on Cowpen's field,
Show'd Southern force could make a braggart
    yield ;
King's Mountain's hights proclaimed in bloody
    words
The value of stanch hearts and Southern swords ;
And Valley Forge, if it had tongues, might speak
Of sufferings that would blanch the stoutest cheek,

Endured for *love of country*, by the brave,
True Southern tide of that almighty wave
That was to roll above and free the land
Of a despotic kingdom's hireling band
Of mercenaries.

        Say, my brethren, say,
Are we less true to freedom's cause to-day,
Than we were then ?   Think you that brows that
    spurned
Control from parent hand, and proudly turned
From mother England when she grew unjust,
Will bend to those who have betrayed the trust
Reposed in them ?   Altho' a kindred tie
Unites us all, too deep within us lie
The seeds implanted by our fathers bold,
To guard our rights e'en from a brother's hold,
If he encroaches on the limits set
When justice and equality have met
To guard them.   Think of this, 't is all we ask;
You then will see how odious the task
That you have voluntarily assumed,
Must in our eyes appear.   You have presumed
Too far, and if you 're just you 'll own to this,
Nor rashly push the matter till there is

No honorable path left for the South
But to withdraw herself from the cold mouth
That with a Judas' kiss would thus betray
Its country; for the hope of power and sway
That may be gained if the South yields her
    right,
Is the true motive of your dastard fight!
    Ah! this is a sad picture, and it pains
My heart to paint it.   Surely there remains
Some brightening tints to gild the portrait dark?
Some flashes of a clearer, holier spark
That latent lies within fraternal breasts,
To glow and radiate when the kindling tests
Are tried, of partings that will wring the heart
(If the South takes the firm resolve to part
Rather than lie down bleeding at the feet
Of Northern despotism)?   Then will meet
Sons, fathers, brothers, to unlink the chain
By Nature riveted, but rent in twain
By goading malice under friendly guise!
O! ere that clouded dawn shall darkly rise
O'er our loved land, will not some patriot soul
Step forth to turn the scales?   Nor let the foul
And parricidal act be hastened on

By the base means that heretofore have done
The insidious work.

     O ! could I speak
The thoughts that wring my heart and blanch my
  cheek,
I'd surely prove to ye, my brothers, all,
How great will be our honored country's fall
If such a consummation of wild schemes
Is wrought beneath our day-star's sacred beams.
Were I but blessed with angel eloquence,
I'd send a stream of light convergent hence
To reach the holy sanctuary within
Each heart, and show the heinous, monstrous sin
That ye are perpetrating, all ye hosts
Of instigators—who now make your boasts
Of having gained the day for which ye've striven
To crush your brethren's rights before High
  Heaven !
Can ye not see the ill ye've surely wrought?
Do ye not force an act whose memory—fraught
With vain repinings and regrets, too late—
Will blacken all your future's somber fate ?
Down, down Dictation ! cease your grinding rules,
Which only cowards yield to, knaves, or fools.

You vainly strive on Freedom's neck your yoke
To place; it bends not—but it may be broke
And in its shattered fragments you will find
But wild remorse, for having rashly twin'd
A cord to strangle Liberty's sweet breath,
And caused your country's dark, dishonored
    death!
  O! here, where ambient skies and balmy airs
Distill etherial mildness—nature wears
Perennial verdure, and great hearts expand
Beneath her genial influence, strong yet bland—
Think you, our Southern blood thrills not as true
With patriotism, and leaps up anew,
Indignant at oppression, as with *you,*
Girt with a chilling atmosphere of frost
In which vitality is almost lost?
Think you, the bounteousness here spread abroad
By an all-powerful and generous God,
Wakes in our warm hearts no responsive swell
To him, who with abundance, shows how well
He recompenses our fidelity,
In honoring his most wise and just decree,
By giving each thing its own proper place
In this progressive, onward, upward race?

Ay, ready hearts and willing hands here strive
To keep the sacred flame of Truth alive
Upon the altar of just principle;
Whose maxims holy and invincible,
Are graved too deeply to be e'er erased
By partisan scurrility, tho' graced
With theologian dogmas, which but show
Religion never yet was made to go
With politics.   Here, no professions we
E'er make—here 's no self-righteous Pharisee—
We own we 're *human*, and as such, oft err;
Yet still, one rule finds ready worshiper
In all : To strive to do to others as
We 'd have them do to us!
                              Now this, alas!
Seems blotted from our Northern brethren's
      code;
And, as companions on *their upward* (!) road,
They cherish hatred, animosity,
And vent in petty spites, antipathy
To all our institutions; while they raise
A standard of their own for prayer and praise,
And climb to heaven upon the sins of all
They 've trampled on this sin-provoking ball!

No doubt we have a heathenish look com-
    pared
To them, for we have never wildly shared
In the excitement by false prophets raised—
Uniquely showing how God may be praised,
By desecrating every moral law,
And finding in each physical, a flaw!
We know our soil is not congenial to
This fungus growth; and we're content to go
Along the plainer track of common sense,
Nor yield to every doubtful, wild pretense,
By fanatics set forth to justify
Their measures—while they scoffingly defy
Their country and their Maker, and insist
That truth lies at the bottom of each "ist"
And "ism." Hence, we've seen, how quick the
    growth
Of these monstrosities at the far North,
And "free love," "Mormonism," and their train
Of untold evils, have progressed amain
Thro'out the land, until 't would seem, indeed,
That the "Sixth Angel," mentioned in the creed
Of Revelation, had his wrath poured out,
And "unclean spirits, like to frogs, come out

The Dragon's mouth, and the mouth of the Beast,
And the mouth of the false Prophet." Such, at
    least,
These vile productions of distorted faith
Seem, in their heinous properties, whose breath
Sullies the face of Truth's pure mirror, while
The foul streams pour libations rank and vile,
To overrun and to pollute the land
With the dark scum rising on Error's strand,
And drifting inward, with its tidal might,
To quench Religion's holy, sacred light!
    Ah! true religion, based on charity,
So far exceeds such vile barbarity,
That a comparison between them ne'er
May be attempted on our mundane sphere;
For we would not pollute a shrine so pure
By mingling with its music the harsh roar
Of wolves and lions, to attest its power
Harmonious over discord's angry dower.
But, would we seek for the blessed spot on
    earth
Where this most holy cause has ne'er a dearth
Of followers—we'll find that sacred spot
To be, where bigotry leaves not a blot

To sully the fair face of tolerance;
Where love of man does love of God enhance;
Where nature's beauties are enjoyed by all
As gifts from Heaven, and no dull, leaden pall
Is laid o'er innocent amusement to invest
Sweet holiness with terror—as, when drest
In sackcloth, it must ever seem a gnome,
To lead the young to a cold, gloomy tomb,
In which their natural gayety must lie
Buried forever from each mortal eye.
Ah! where God's worshiped in *glad* anthems, *there*
Arises truest praise and holiest prayer;
And where man for his brother finds excuse,
If weakness leads him to excess (abuse
Of nature's privileges), in his own
Frail being's foibles—which will still atone
For many errors he mayhap commit—
For we 're expressly told, we may not sit
In judgment on each other, lest we be
Judged by a like imperative decree.
'T is only where all *kindly* feelings thrive,
That piety's pure spark is kept alive;
Where love and charity lend their whole strength,
To fan it, till a steady flame at length,

16

It mounts to heaven from altar pure and true,
Which no fanatic stain may e'er imbrue
With oversteeped discolorings from the fount
Where falsehood bubbles and doubt's vapors mount.

There *is* a land where happiness thus reigns
Without the clog of all the clanking chains
In darkness forged. Wouldst find it?   Seek it
    HERE!
We've room for millions, and you need not fear
To test our Southern hospitality.
Warm hearts are beating where each small degree
Of latitude but brings us nearer to
The fount of warmth, the source of light, the true
Inspirer of each ardent impulse—he
By all acknowledged day's divinity,
Great Sol! who broad dispenses loving smiles
To teach us mortals how sweet faith beguiles
Dark doubt of all its harsh incrustings, in
Thus lovingly enfolding earth to win
The treasures buried deeply in her heart,
Which his warm, generous smile of trust, will
    start
To life and bloom; but which 'neath chilling blast
Of doubting wind, their tender leaves would cast;

Put forth no buds of promise, but fall dead,
Because kind influence was not around them shed!
But faith and kindness here go hand in hand;
Come! tho' your prejudices *North* may stand,
Yet *here, once here*, they must, they *will* give way
Before the clearer beam, the brighter day
Poured from our tropic sun's enlightening ray!
    When once amongst us, you will find how much
Of confidence is to be placed in such
Distorted statements as your "shriekers" give.
Their trade ignores the text, "Live and let live,"
For not content with living their own way,
They'd change the mode of those more blest than
        they
Are; while their practice contradicts in full
Their precept—as one must be very dull
Not to perceive how ill equality
With Blacks, sits on their puffy dignity!
Cuffy does very well to groan about,
But when he comes *too near*, he's put to rout;
And, as a freeman, in a freesoil state,
Experiences far greater slights than wait
Him here, where he is kindly cared for, and
Warm sympathy excites on every hand.

For tho' a slave, he 's human, still, and shares
His master's bounty; while he 'scapes his cares;
And is regarded in each household band
As member of the family.   No hand
Disdains his proffered grasp, no children there
Refuse their love and kiss with him to share;
And "*Mammy*" is a queen-bee in each hive
For subjects, White and Black, to proudly strive
Who shall with greatest honors load her down!
Would not your free-soil matrons shrink and
        frown
To see their infant rose-buds clinging round
These sooty goddesses in nursery crowned?
And yet you prate equality tho' blind
To all its bearings !
                        We 've, you see, divined
How far your equalizing process goes:
You 'd like to crush those you regard as foes,
Because they differ in opinion; and
The readiest means to do so, you command.
Poor Sambo 's dragged from quietude to be
Your shield, and in the warfare gets, we see,
The wounds—for you but cause his owner to
Curtail his privileges, and to go

To greater lengths, more rigid means to save
His property from felon's grasp. You have
Thus heaped upon *us all*, both White and Black,
Annoyance, and in this you draw not back;
And why, why do you do this thing? ·To be,
We answer, rulers, lords of all you see!
For prating kindness does not come to *acts;*
The Negro finds he has to deal with *facts,*
Cold, stubborn facts, when on your soil he learns
His stanch adviser, promised friend, now spurns
His *brotherly* regard, and turns his back
When funds and labor both are getting slack,
And the poor outcast, who has birthright sold,
Finds out, too late, *the pottage is all cold !*

Ah! better, would you kindly with us join
To polish this neglected, barbarous coin,
So that the metal may ring bright and clear
Upon Truth's pure and sympathetic ear.
You'd help the Negro's progress more, far more,
By bringing him to our enlightened shore,
And teaching him the way to better things
Beneath our Eagle's broad, protecting wings!
But still it would not do to leave him *free,*
Even in this fair land of liberty—

Because he would not make a proper use
Of freedom, and 't would be to him a curse
Rather than a blessing.   Then let him be
A slave, if by such wholesome slavery
We free him from a bondage worse, more dire—
A chain that shackles intellect's pure fire—
A mental thralldom in which heart and soul
Together in the mire of darkness roll,
In savagism's deep Egyptian night,
Denied blest Christianity's clear light,
And burying the seal by God imprest,
'Neath monstrous barbarisms, foul, unblest!
Think you he'll progress on his native soil?
And is he *injured* when we make him toil?
God ne'er designed that man should be supine—
He gives us means, and we must thence divine
How to exert them; and when powers exist
In others, wrapt in barbarism's mist,
Do we not act the good Samaritan
In freeing them from the unholy ban
That lays a leaden clog upon their might,
And steeps them in the darkness of midnight?
Say, are we not the Negro's *truest friends?*
And are we not the source, 'neath God, which sends

A dawning light thro' his benighted soul,
To help it gain the hights where ceaseless roll
Hosannas glorious and anthems grand,
From all who man's condition understand?
  Then bury animosities, my friends!
Contest no law which in its bearing tends
To elevate a poor, unhappy race,
And gives to them in human grade their place.
We *all* are pigmies in the sight of Him
Who fashioned us from nothing! If we swim
Time's ocean with the means that He has given,
'T will land us on the blissful shores of heaven!
And while with greater force *we* breast the wave,
'T will not retard us if we seek to save
Our weaker comrades from the billow's might
That threatens darkness and eternal night.
If we would hasten on that glorious time
Foretold in Holy Writ—when every clime
" Shall own Messiah's name," shall be set free
From savage bonds and all idolatry—
We 'll hesitate not to employ all ways
By which this brightest ending of dark days
May be attained. Be sure the day *will* come
When all will strive to reach that better home;

That " house not made by hands, eternal in
The heavens!" O! what a blessed goal to win!
O! what a glorious birthright, there to be
Progressing still thro' all eternity,
From knowledge unto wisdom, and from love
To adoration, in those courts above,
Where shining seraphs vail their faces pure
While in His presence, whom they rapt adore;
And winged aspirations ceaseless rise
To glories brightening in celestial skies!
    And this is man's immortal destiny.
O, fellow mortals! why not strive to be
Worthy its blessed privileges! and
Disgrace not this our own, our favored land,
That has thus far, triumphant led the van
To better things—by arming, man to man,
To wrangle on a point which ne'er should be
Made pretext for this civil anarchy.
But, as a band of brothers, strive to find
The RIGHT *with mildness*—bear this still in mind;
And where ye differ in opinion, pray
Let Justice be the umpire in the fray;
And meet on *equal* grounds, that each may be
Vested alike with true authority;

Then for the issue—trust to God! He'll hold
The crucible to test the purer gold,
And all that's mingled with alloy, or base,
Must to the finer yield its fitting place!
   Then will sweet Peace, now frightened from
      her nest,
Descend again to regions she loves best;
Then will our Eagle from his eyry high,
Gaze proudly at his rival's blazing eye
That from a higher hight lights all the sky,
And plume its pinions for a greater flight
Than it e'er dreamed of thro' the low'ring night;
Then will our Spangled Banner proudly wave
Above the land where dwell the free and brave;
Then will our Nation's great heart, free from pain,
Throb with contentment's sacred pulse again;
And from Atlantic's to Pacific's shore,
From Mexico's broad gulf, Niagara's roar,
The sounding anthems shall roll glad and free,
Chanting the praise of glorious Liberty,
To swell the pæans of the hosts who day
And night rest not, but ever ceaseless say,
"O! holy, holy, holy Lord!" alway.
   17

Valedictory.

ERE we part, my kind readers, I beg you 'll
    permit
Me a few words on leaving:
                    You may not see fit
To indorse all the sentiments I have expressed,
But my motive, you still must acknowledge, the
    best
That could have inspired a lover of peace,
And hater of falsehood's base, spurious increase,
That of late years has peopled the pulpit and
    press,
The forum and Senate with fatal excess;
And spread its vile progeny over the face
Of our once happy country, to sully, debase,
And exterminate wholesome and practical laws,
And crush our dear liberty in its huge jaws.

    To you, the pure-hearted and brave of our land,
Who the rights of each brother full well under-
    stand,

I need not appeal; for the monitor blest,
That holds its own court in each true patriot's
    breast,
Shall with eloquence speak, and your actions
    control,
In all matters relating to body and soul;
And raise warning finger, if, even in thought,
You'd seek to presume on the privilege bought
At so countless a price, by our forefathers brave,
Their country to liberate, ransom and save
From the deep degradation of despotic rule,
Whose precepts are grafted in tyranny's school.
Let your hearts be the balance in which you will
    weigh
The matters that ask your opinion to-day;
We fear not the verdict such jurymen just
Will return in the case, and our cause freely trust
To your reason, humanity, wisdom, and skill,
Which the *right* will discern in spite of ill-will,
With its witnesses bribed to distort the truth fair,
Till its bloated proportions make simple folks
    stare!
Now our case, as it stands, you have heard me
    rehearse;

I condensed it to suit the design of my verse,
That you may discern but its rights and its
    wrongs,
And give that impartial return which belongs,
We know, to each matter that's fairly discussed
By equity's arguments, honest and just.
   I have drawn no false pictures to work on your
    sense,
And excite a deep sympathy by such pretense—
I leave *that* field open to one Mistress S—we,
Who's better provided the journey to go.
As for me, I'm not fitted to grope in the dark,
But prefer the least glimmer of truth's faintest
    spark,
To that Egyptian darkness which fancy can fill
To suit morbid appetites, strengthen ill-will,
And work out the ends of dictation, without
The least ray to show the poor traveler the
    route
Which his guide (who, bat-like, sees a way thro'
    the gloom,
That will place all opposers beneath a cold tomb),
Is leading him on, over quagmire and bog
His reason to deaden, his ideas to clog,

While breathing things monstrous and foul in his
    ear,
To harrow his feelings or thrill him with fear,
Till mystified, horrified, not knowing why,
He joins in the wild and fanatical cry,
And rushes to battle 'gainst all who resist
The allurements that lie in romance's thick
    mist,
And prefer common sense and experience's tests
To the fallacies which this base medium invests
With colors prismatic to catch simple eyes,
But which the discerning detect as the dyes
Of falsehood, that garbs with the semblance of
    truth
The creatures of fiction, to cheat age and youth.
   No, not by such means do I seek to impose
Upon any; the road's alike open to foes
As to friends, all its windings and turnings to
    trace ;
And for traveling companion, plain Truth's honest
    face,
At their elbow they'll find thro' the whole of the
    route,
To clear each obstruction, dissolve every doubt,

And radiate beams from the Fountain of light,
To exorcise demons begotten of fright,
Who hold the perceptions of all who give ear
To raving disturbers of harmony's sphere!
O! call not that soul, true philanthropy's seat,
That sows seeds of discord at each brother's feet,
Where the fast-growing tares check each kindlier
*   growth,*
And ripen to hatred's rank blossoms with both.

   A word to reformers: Before you begin
To parade to the public each light, floating sin
That skims on the stream of your neighbor's warm
     life,
Would it not be as well to allay every strife,
Every wrong and oppression that broods o'er
     your own
Household hearths, or stalks thro' your land, with
     a tone
Of despair, calling loudly for work and for bread,
From *free* operatives?   As well, would you
     shed
A portion of light (where you've so much to
     spare),
To help to relieve your own poor of their care?

As for us, thanks to God! want's unknown in our
   clime,
Our workers, tho' slaves, ring a merrier chime,
On the bells that pour forth the fleet progress of
   Time!
Your laborer is *White, and your equal*—yet he
Is a sufferer to a much greater degree
Than his ebony rival—tho' this till doomsday
Perhaps you'll contend; but I've this much to
   say:
Let "crises," "panics," "suspensions," invade
And break down the barriers guarding all trade;
Let banks go to ruin, and stocks sink to naught,
The whirlpool, to one class with misery fraught,
Glides light past the other as singing brooks play
In the beams of the sun on a calm summer's day;
And while "factory strikes," 'mong your suffering
   poor,
Tell too plainly the wolf's at each working man's
   door;
Our careless, light-hearted, and good-natured
   "Cuff,"
With his sleek, glossy hide, shows he's still got
   enough

And to spare, should some poor Northern White
    brother need
To share his snug cabin, his garment and feed.
    Why bring in the aid of the novelist's pen
To work on the feelings of warm-hearted men,
By dressing in pitiful guise every gross
Misrepresentation? We 're not at a loss
For *facts and hard truths*, when we enter *your*
    door,
To substantiate all we assert of your poor;
Nor need we the pallet of fancy, to paint
How near to a sinner comes every saint
Who bellows from pulpit invective and jeer
To stir up antipathy in each compeer,
And trumpet contention abroad with *that* Word
That the olive should tender instead of the sword.
For Religion should bind with sweet charity's
    clasp,
Not nurse in its flowers the sting of the asp;
But gently diffuse its etherial balm,
Each discord to soften, each tempest to calm.
    There may be some cases (which all must de-
      plore),
Of cruel injustice and wrong done the poor

Negro slave; this I've candor to own. Yet I still
Ask, are *any* exempt from such ill?
Are there none in *your* midst, at this moment,
    opprest
By grinding exactitude, heartless, at best,
'Mong your *White* operatives? Say, do they not
    give
Their heart's blood for pittance which scarce lets
    them live?
Ah, Pharisees! ere you the Publican spurn,
Look at home; to your own moral grievances turn;
Cleanse the leprosies foul that within you exist,
Till no longer you see thro' a 'wildering mist,
Ere you lay your cold hands where your heart
    ought to be,
And whine out your thanks, that you are not as he.
    Let charity, with you, begin in your home,
Fit subjects 't will find, and no longer need roam
On a wild, thankless mission, devoid of all grace,
Which mistakes both the calling, the time, and the
    place,
In its useless endeavors to draw forth the mote
From its neighbor's clear vision, which fails not
    to note

The broad beam obstructing the visual ray
Of the optics of those who would point out the
way·
To the better perceptions of others they 'd guide,
And swamp friend and foe in a treacherous tide,
Rising slowly and surely where'er it finds room,
To ingulf all the nation within a cold tomb.
  Pray, pray for more light, from the Fountain
    above,
Till its glory doth flood all your souls with pure
  love,
Not only for him, the Creator of all,
But for man, *his* creation upon this dun ball!
For once you but cherish a sympathy sweet,
For each human waif on Time's ocean you meet,
And kindly admonish him when he doth err,
Yet *love hin thro' all things*, let radiance or blur
On his brow leave a mark for distinction or shame—
Still, but cherish for him an undying flame
Of holy forbearance to guide thro' all gloom,
And from error's waste lead to the brightness and
  bloom
Of truth and of purity, you will achieve
A power, for which you 'll have no cause to grieve;

A power of persuasion, the mild and the true,
That will gently, yet surely, prevail where the crew
Of force, domineering, can never gain ground,
Tho' policy girt it with piety round.
An enemy may be by kindness o'ercome,
And soft words will make the wrathful man dumb.
You should not abuse theological power,
By pointing its shafts at your neighbor's home-
  bower,
And poisoning the darts in dark sophistry's pool,
Thus making religion a puppet and tool,
Thro' whose channel your venomed ill-nature may
  flow
'Gainst all who but differ from you here below.
  The pulpit, the Holy of Holies should be!
There, questions political, all anarchy,
Should be banished—its calling's more sacred, by
  far,
Than leading a caucus or waging a war;
'T is God's throne on earth! (or rather, *should be*,
But man has polluted the pure sanctuary);
And should not be defiled by such streams as
  to-day
In muddy disturbances take their dark way

From this fountain, thus basely turned out of its
    course,
To babble with bigots who scream themselves
    hoarse
While fiercely contending 'gainst nature's pure
    laws,
To uphold an ill-grounded, fanatical cause !
    I would say to ye all, ye Reformers so bold,
Who enter, unasked, our Southern stronghold—
Should ye need a *new* field for a famous display
Of rhetorical powers and windy array,
Turn your weapons, so logical, on your own
    band
Of clerical wranglers—for all understand
That *they need reforming the most in our land!*
They seem to forget that their mission is " peace!"
And, lion-like, roar from their soft waving fleece
Till one is in doubt whether sheep-cot, or lair,
Is appropriate term for God's temple fair!
    And now to my friends, and *the rest of mankind,*
I have something to say. We have, all of us,
    shrined
In our heart's secret chamber, some idol—tho'
    blind

We may be to the knowledge, yet others can see
What to us is obscure to the latest degree;
With one, 't is ambition—another, 't is love—
And a third worships Mammon, all creatures above;
While some, purer hearted, (alas! they are few!)
Throne Truth there, with radiance to shine out
    anew
O'er each fallacy bred in dark Error's abode,
To obstruct and obscure every newly-laid road
That invites earthly tourist to take shorter route
When seeking some knotty point's flaws to find out.
Then again, other hearts cling to Error, and hug
Her delusions, not knowing how vainly they tug
At a chain that coils firmer the harder they pull,
And binds their perceptions with leaden clog dull.
And still, other deities, other hearts own
Unconsciously—yet, by their fruits they are known;
And so I appeal to your reason and sense
To judge between truth and fallacious pretense.
My motive I feel to be honest and true,
In submitting these arguments freely to you;
And if I have blindly advanced a false cause
'T will quickly be seen, when, with Nature's known
    laws

'Tis compared.   All I ask, is impartial survey
Of *both sides* of this mighty question to-day—
Give *each* a fair hearing, and when you do this
Be sure you're not swayed by the sheer fallacies
Set forth by the novelist but to confound
Your reason, and lead you o'er treacherous ground;
But lay aside romance and take *solid fact*,
If you would arrive at conclusion exact;
Nor weep over Fiction's all-fanciful wrongs,
But give your sweet sympathy where it belongs,
When actual experience proves to your mind
That sufferings and wrongs exist 'mong your
     kind.
   In this age of free thought we have, each one,
     a right
To investigate aught that seems dim to our sight;
And when we've arrived at conclusions, we still
Can express them, I hope, without rousing ill-
     will.
I've simply expressed what I think to be true,
And if in opinion I differ from you,
We do but what mortals will everywhere do,
For few think alike on all points—yet on *this*
I would ask you to pause before you dismiss

The matter entirely—give it a thought—
'Tis by *thinking* most wonderful changes are
    wrought!
For Thought is the mine from which was exterred
All the wonders that nations entranced have heard;
In its depths the great giant was molded to form
When he rose in a vaporous moisture so warm
From his kettle-bed, which the boy dreamily eyed
As the slight curling breath pushed the thick lid
    aside,
And saw in the action a slumbering power,
That works mighty levers at this present hour!
'T was from Thought's deep recesses that Franklin
    brought forth
The bright spark electric, whose magical worth
The world now attests, as it girdles the North,
Spans the soft breezy South, clasps the East and
    the West,
And draws nations nearer in unity blest!
For, from Heaven the spark came to circle the
    Earth,
And herald a new and a glorious birth
In the fair field of Progress, to show forth to man
How much he may grasp with an up-reaching span

That not vainly aspires, if a pure motive gives
The impetus!

       So, then, fare ye well! If there lives
But a spark of true patriotism still in our land,
I fear not the Union will yet firmly stand,
The bulwark of Liberty! which the harsh gale
Of partisan violence, tho' it assail,
May storm round in vain — for its true heart of
    oak
Will resist to the last the dastardly stroke,
And ride out the tempest with sails all unriven,
And furl but its flag on the bright shores of
    Heaven!

Notes.

Notes.

PROGRESSION.—In taking the Nebular Hypothesis as my argument for creation, I but agree with many learned writers and astronomers. But my attention was chiefly called to the subject of Progression, by a perusal of a little volume entitled, *Vestiges of the Natural History of Creation*, by —— Mantell. I have endeavored (as far as in me lies the power) to carry out the ideas of the author of that work—for I most religiously believe them to be correct—and cordially recommend the perusal of that book to every one desirous of an intellectual feast. There is certainly no work, of the same number of pages, that contains the same amount of information. It is a clear embodiment of the *Multum in Parvo*, so desirable in all writings.

As far as the slavery question is concerned, I have acted for "conscience sake"—and think, while so doing, I but echo the sentiments of all calm reasoners and lovers of truth, North, South, East, or West.

Page 17.

—— *The mighty Word which was*
In the beginning.

"In the beginning was the Word, and the Word was with God, and the Word was God."—St. John i : 1.

Page 19.

O! wondrous sight, a universe all fire!

"The nebulous matter of space, previous to the formation of stellar and planetary bodies, must have been a universal Fire Mist; an idea which we can scarcely comprehend, though the reasons for arriving at it seem irresistible."— *Vestiges of Creation, p.* 20.

Page 21.

And still another law have we to show.

"Now, mechanical philosophy informs us that the instant a mass begins to rotate, there is generated a tendency to fling off its outer portions. In other words, the law of centrifugal force begins to operate. There are, then, two forces acting in opposition to each other, the one attracting *to*, the other throwing *from* the center. While these remain exactly counterpoised, the mass necessarily continues entire; but the least excess of the centrifugal over the attractive force would be attended with the effect of separating the mass and its outer parts. These outer parts would then be left as a ring round the central body, which ring would continue to revolve with the velocity possessed by the central mass at the moment of separation, but not necessarily participating in any changes afterwards undergone by that body. This is a process which might be repeated as soon as a new

excess arose in the centrifugal over the attractive forces
working in the parent mass. It might, indeed, continue
to be repeated, until the mass attained the ultimate limits
of the condensation which its constitution imposed upon
it. From what cause might arise the periodical occurrence
of an excess of the centrifugal force? If we suppose the
agglomeration of a nebulous mass to be a process attended
by refrigeration or cooling, which many facts render likely,
we can easily understand why the outer parts, hardening
under this process, might, by virtue of the greater solidity
thence acquired, begin to present some resistance to the
attractive force. As the solidification proceeded, this resistance would become greater, though there would still be
a tendency to adhere. Meanwhile, the condensation of the
central mass would be going on, tending to produce a separation from what may now be termed the *solidifying
crust.* During the contention between the attractions of
these two bodies, or parts of one body, there would probably be a ring of attenuation between the mass and its crust.
At length, when the central mass had reached a certain
stage in its advance toward solidification, a separation
would take place, and the crust would become a detached
ring. It is clear, of course, that some law, presiding over
the refrigeration of heated gaseous bodies, would determine
the stages at which rings were thus formed and detached.
We do not know any such law, but what we have seen as-
sures us it is one observing, and reducible to, mathematical
formula.

"If these rings consisted of matter nearly uniform throughout, they would probably continue each in its original form; but there are many chances against their being uniform in constitution. The unavoidable effect of irregularity in their constitution, would be to cause them to gather toward centers of superior solidity, by which the annular form would, of course, be destroyed. The ring would, in short, break into several masses, the largest of which would be likely to attract the lesser into itself. The whole mass would then necessarily settle into a spherical form, by virtue of the law of gravitation; in short, would then become a planet revolving round the sun. Its rotary motion would, of course, continue, and satellites might then be thrown off in turn, from its body, in exactly the same way as the primary planets had been thrown off from the sun. The rule, if I can be allowed so to call it, receives a striking support from what appears to be its exceptions. While there are many chances against the matter of the rings being sufficiently equable to remain in the annular form till they were consolidated, it might nevertheless be otherwise in some instances: that is to say, the equableness might, in those instances, be sufficiently great. Such was probably the case with the two rings around the body of Saturn, which remain a living picture of the arrangement, if not the condition, in which all the planetary masses at one time stood. It may also be admitted that, when a ring broke up, it was possible that the fragments might spherify separately. Such seems to be the actual history of the ring between Jupiter and Mars, in whose place we now find four* planets, much beneath the smallest of the rest in size, and moving nearly at the same distance from the sun, though in orbits so elliptical, and of such different planes, that they keep apart."—*Vestiges of Creation, p.* 11.

Page 22.

——*The same power by which apples fall.*

The law of gravitation.

Page 23.

For, once, a circling mass of liquid fire,
Our sun filled all our system's space, entire.

" I may here, also, remind the reader that there are other grounds for this hypothesis, besides observations on the nebulæ. Overlooking the zodiacal light, which has been thought a residuum of the nebulous fluid of our system, we find geology taking us back *toward* a state of our globe which can not otherwise be explained. It was clearly, at one time, in a state of igneous fluidity—the state in which its oblately spheroidal form was assumed under the law of centrifugal force. Since then it has cooled, at least in the exterior crust. We thus have it passing through a chemical process, attended by dimin-

* Modern research has discovered over *fifty* small planets in this space.

ishing heat. Whence the heat at first, if not from the
causes indicated in the nebular hypothesis? But this
is not all. In looking back along the steps of such a process, we have no limit imposed. There is nothing to call
for our stopping, till we reach one of those extreme tem-
peratures which would vaporize the solid materials; and
this gives us exactly that condition of things which is
implied by the nebular cosmogony."—*Vestiges of Creation,*
p. 209.

Page 39.

Where earth's diameter exceeds, 't is known,
Its polar depth, and proves our planet's form
To be an oblate spheroid.

"Although it appears, from the preceding facts, that
the earth is spherical, yet it is not a perfect sphere. If
it were, the length of the degrees of latitude, from the
equator to the poles, would be uniformly the same; but
it has been found, by the most careful measurement, that
as we go from the equator toward the poles, the length
increases with the latitude.

"These measurements have been made by the most
eminent mathematicians of different countries, and in
various places, from the equator to the arctic circle.
They have found that a degree of latitude at the arctic
circle was *nine-sixteenths* of a mile longer than a degree
at the equator, and that the ratio of increase for the inter-

mediate degrees was nearly as the sines of the latitude. Thus the theory of Sir Isaac Newton was confirmed, that the body of the earth was more rounded and convex between the tropics, but considerably flattened at the poles." *Geography of the Heavens and Class-Book of Astronomy, by Elijah H. Burritt.*

Page 39.

——*A residuum*
Of that great heat which kept vaporiform
All matter in times past.

See Baron Fourier's *Théorie Analytique de la Chaleur.* 1822.

Page 41.

——*For where the cup*
Of mighty seas sunk deep within her breast
(*Deeper than those which now within it rest*),
Granitic mountains reared their scraggy heads.

"Geology tells us as plainly as possible, that the original crystalline mass was not a perfectly smooth ball, with air and water playing round it. There were vast irregularities in the surface—irregularities trifling, perhaps, compared with the whole bulk of the globe, but assuredly vast in comparison with any which now exist upon it. These irregularities might be occasioned by inequalities in the cooling of the substance, or by accidental and local slug-

19

gishness of the materials, or by local effects of the con-
centrated internal heat. From whatever cause they arose,
there they were, enormous granitic mountains, interspersed
with seas which sunk to a depth equally profound, and
by which, perhaps, the mountains were wholly or partially
covered.   *   *   *   *   *   *   *   *
There is the clearest evidence that the seas of those days
were not, in some instances, less than a hundred miles in
depth, however much more. The subaqueous mountains
must necessarily have been of at least equal magnitude."—
Vestiges of Creation, p. 29.

Page 43.

And what this substance?   Carbon—known to be
Of herb and plant the main commodity.

"Limestone is a carbonate of lime, a secondary compound, of which one of the ingredients, carbonic acid gas,
presents the element *carbon*, a perfect novelty in our progress. Whence this substance? The question is the more
interesting, from our knowing that carbon is the main
ingredient in organic things. There is reason to believe
that its primeval condition was that of a gas, confined in
the interior of the earth, and diffused in the atmosphere.
The atmosphere still contains about a two-thousandth part
of carbonic acid gas, forming the grand store from which
the substance of each year's crop of herbage and grain is
derived, passing from herbage and grain into animal
substance, and from animals again rendered back to the

atmosphere in their expired breath, so that its amount is never impaired. Knowing this, when we hear of carbon beginning to appear in the ascending series of rocks, we are unavoidably led to consider it as marking a time of some importance in the earth's history, a new era of natural conditions, one in which organic life has probably played a part."— *Vestiges of Creation, p. 31.*

Page 46.

―― *Geology doth show*
Hundreds of species in this strata low.

" Upward of three hundred species of plants have been ascertained to exist in the coal formation; but it is not necessary to suppose that the whole contained in that system are now, or will be, distinguished. * * * * Coal strata are nearly confined to the group termed the carboniferous formation. Thin beds are not unknown afterward, but they occur only as a rare exception. It is therefore thought that the most important of the conditions which allowed of so abundant a terrestial vegetation, had ceased about the time when this formation was closed."— *Vestiges of Creation, pp. 45, 49.*

Page 47.

Behold ! the forms to which was given birth
Spontaneous—in creatures made to be
Dwellers alike of either land or sea !

" These animals are of the vertebrate sub-kingdom, but

of its lowest class next after fishes—namely: reptiles—a portion of the terrestial tribes, whose imperfect respiratory system, perhaps, fitted them for enduring an atmosphere not yet quite suitable for birds or mammifers. The specimens found in the muschelkalk are allied to the crocodile and lizard tribes of the present day; but, in the latter instance, are upon a scale of magnitude as much superior to present forms, as the lepidodendron of the coal era was superior to the dwarf club-mosses of our time. These saurians also combine some peculiarities of a most extraordinary character.

" The animal to which the name *ichthyosaurus* has been given, was as long as a young whale, and it was fitted for living in the water, though breathing the atmosphere. It had the vertebral column and general bodily form of a fish, but to that were added the head and breastbone of a lizard, and the paddles of the whale tribes. The beak, moreover, was that of a porpoise, and the teeth were those of a crocodile. It must have been a most destructive creature to the fish of those early seas.

" The *plesiosaurus* was of similar bulk, with a turtle-like body and paddles, showing that the sea was its element; but with a long, serpent-like neck, terminating in a saurian head, calculated to reach prey at a considerable distance. These two animals, of which many varieties have been discovered, constituting distinct species, are supposed to have lived in the shallow borders of the seas of this and subsequent formations, devouring immense

quantities of the finny tribes. It was at first thought
that no creatures approaching them in character now
inhabit the earth; but, latterly, Mr. Darwin has discovered,
in the reptile-peopled Gallapagos Islands, in the South
Sea, a marine saurian, from three to four feet long.

"The *megalosaurus* was an enormous lizard—a land
creature, also carnivorous. The *pterodactyle* was another
lizard, but furnished with wings to pursue its prey in the
air, and varying in size between a cormorant and a snipe.
Crocodiles abounded, and some of these were herbivorous.
Such was the iguanodon, a creature of the character of
the iguana of the Ganges, but reaching a hundred feet in
length, or twenty times that of its modern representative.

"There were also numerous *tortoises*, some of them
reaching a great size; and Professor Owen has found in
Warwickshire some remains of an animal of the batrachian
order (the order to which frogs and toads belong), to which,
from the peculiar form of the teeth, he has give the name
of labyrinthidon. Thus, three of Cuvier's four orders of
reptilia (*sauria*, *chelonia*, and *batrachia*) are represented
in this formation, the serpent order (*ophidia*) being alone
wanting."—*Vestiges of Creation, p.* 52.

Page 49.
——*Thus, link by link, to fill*
The gap between the earliest formed and man.

"Such is the outline of the fauna of the tertiary era,
as ascertained by the illustrious naturalists who first

devoted their attention to it. It will be observed, that it brings us up to the felinæ, or carnivora, a considerably elevated point in the animal scale, but still leaving a blank for the quadrumana (monkeys) and for man, who collectively form, as will afterward be seen, the first group in that scale."—*Vestiges of Creation, p.* 69.

Page 67.

The physiologist observes, each animal
Progresses still, while in the germinal,
Thro' changes, all resembling the forms
Of lower orders in the scale.

See the Scale of Nature, in *Fletcher's Rudiments of Physiology.*

Page 96.

Once spake that country's savior next to God.

"And let me conjure you, in the name of our common country, as you value your own sacred honor, as you respect the rights of humanity, and as you regard the military and national character of America, to express your utmost horror and detestation of the man who wishes, under any specious pretenses, to overturn the liberties of our country ; and who wickedly attempts to open the floodgates of civil discord, and deluge our rising empire in blood."—*Washington's speech to his officers, on the occasion of the "Newburgh addresses."*

Page 106.

That slavery was authorized by law
Among the Israelites, etc.

"The Hebrews had several kinds of servants. Some were mere slaves for life, and were sold and disposed of by their masters as they thought fit: such were the strangers bought or taken in war.—Lev. xxv: 44, etc. Such are also called *bodies*, because their masters' rigor reaches only to their body.—Rev. xviii: 13. Hebrew slaves or bond-servants, who could only at first be bound six years, and at the end thereof were to be dismissed, with presents from their masters; but their children, born during their servitude, continued to be their master's property : but if they declined to go free, their master, with an awl, bored their ear to the door-post, as a token they could not afterward have their freedom, at least till the year of jubilee. If a master struck a bond-servant till he died, he was only punished, not condemned to death. If an ox gored to death a bond-servant, the owner paid thirty shekels of silver as his price, and the ox was stoned. If a master struck out the eye of his slave, he was to give him his liberty as a compensation.—Ex. xxi: 1, 11, 20, 26, 27: Deut. xxv: 1, 18."—*From Brown's Dictionary of the Bible.*

Page 134.

I would exclaim, as did a noble one
Of Nature's freemen.

In John Mitchel's reply to the Joint Committee of the Senate and House of Representatives of Louisiana, inviting him to the seat of Government, he says: " You will not condemn nor wonder at the zeal of a stranger and a refugee for that Union. In my case, it is not unnatural. To me, from my childhood, the United States has been a sacred unity—one and indivisible—the completest, grandest achievement and monument of wit and courage of man in modern times. The admiration became a passion; and the passion led me far, and cost me dear; but the dearer it cost me, the more jealously and proudly I cherish now my old faith and hope; now, when the banner I gazed on so long from hopeless distance, with 'the desire of the moth for the star,' gleams and waves above me at last. May the colors of God's bow be torn asunder ere the stripes of that majestic banner."

Page 161.

And even the poor Indians now own
This to be true.

Most of the newspapers of the day have given us accounts of the interview between the President of the United States and the delegations of the Pawnee, Ponca, and Pottawatomie tribes of Indians, on business connected with the Government. I would like to transcribe in full the speech of each "Chief" to his "Grandfather," to show how completely these poor forest children have come to a knowledge of their insignificance, and dependence on a more favored race, but condensation forbids it, so I will content myself with a few extracts.

One said, "My Grandfather, you see me to-day, I am poor. *   *   *   * I think this is a splendid mansion. I think you are like the Great Spirit. Everything the white man makes is wonderful to us. When I see you, and see all these curiosities, I feel as if I am not poor.

Another—"I come here to-day and look about and see your splendid mansion, and it surprises me; but still I know a *white man* can do anything and make anything, and I hope we shall be put in the way to do these things, and not be poor. We have been a long way to see you, and a long time coming here, and, now that we have seen you, it looks as if the Great Spirit is smiling upon us" (alluding to the sunshine and clear sky).

But Wae-gah-sah-pi, or "The Whip," a chief of the Ponca tribe, embodied more truth in a part of his address, than many a more logical white brother might be capable of doing. "My Grandfather," he spake, "I call you Grandfather for no other reason than this: God made me one color, and you of another; but God was partial to you, and made you of a better color. You came into existence and so did I. It was the will of the Great Spirit that we both came into existence. *   *   *   * It was the will of the Great Spirit that made you more powerful than me; it was the will of the Great Spirit that you should take this land from us—this land that you stand on to-day belongs to me. You are a man, my Grandfather, and so am I. Everything that you have made, Grandfather, is worthy of attention—is worthy of looking at."

THE END.